To Sor

James Alfred McCann

Iron Mask Press Richmond BC

DEDICATION

To Jess. For reminding me I still have stories to tell.

Children of Ruin

First Publication by Iron Mask Press 2018.

Paperback: ISBN 978-0-9937486-4-6
eBook: ISBN 978-09937486-3-9
© 2018 by James Alfred McCann.

Edited by Mary Ellen Reid.
Cover Photography by Adobe Images
Interior photography by iStock Photo
Cover design by Jessica Cole www.jesswesley.com

For more information
www.jamesmccann.info

In regione caecorum rex est luscus.

(In the land of the blind, the one-eyed man is king.)

Desiderius Erasmus,

Dutch author, philosopher, & scholar (1466 - 1536)

CHAPTER ONE

No matter how hard I rubbed my hands against my clothes, my stepfather's sons' blood wouldn't wipe off. *It doesn't matter anymore*, I told myself as I stood, exposed, where the trees clustered in open spaces on the outskirts of the dense woods behind me. I spied my only hope to survive—a roadblock of soldiers posted just outside town. I counted seven of them and wrote this down in my notebook. It was important to record everything. Had become important when the army enforced martial law. Ever since the end of the world had been at hand.

Only two arrows left. One stained with the blood of Kyle, my eldest stepbrother. *This one I will save to kill my stepfather.* I put it back into my quiver and took out the unstained arrow. With shaking hands, I nocked it, drew back the bow's string, and inhaled deeply. Once the fletching rested beneath my chin, my shaking stopped. This shot didn't need to kill; it needed to get the soldiers' attention so they'd chase me.

The bow twanged as the arrow released. I turned and fled. Bullets cut through the trees. The soldiers chased me into the woods. I led them toward my home, to where my stepfather was waiting to kill me. I ran until I stood at the edge of the trees, where a small farmhouse sat in the center of an empty field.

"Harbinger!" my stepfather screamed, huddled with a rifle in a roost atop the house. I didn't even know what a harbinger was. "The end times are not coming, they are here!"

The scar that crossed his scalp and cut over his face was visible from where I stood. Even with only his right eye, my stepfather was a flawless sharpshooter. One good shot and I would have been dead. I considered letting the soldiers catch me. But if they did, they would never help me—they would know what I had done. They would know why I had blood on my hands.

"I'm not the child you forced helpless into the woods!" I yelled, taunting him, as I tried again to wipe the blood from my hands.

"Where are my sons?" my stepfather yelled back from the roost. He searched the edge of the woods with the riflescope, and I knew he was waiting for me to show. I spied the open cellar doors just a short sprint away. Was this a trap set by my stepfather in hopes I was stupid enough to make a dash for the shelter?

Thing was, I *was* that stupid.

The soldiers crashed through the bushes as if telling me to act now. If I made a break, zigzagged, my stepfather might miss me. When the military emerged, he'd care more about stopping them than catching me. Surely, self-preservation was greater than his thirst for revenge.

Running with the loaded bow was impossible, so I sheathed the arrow. Then I took a deep breath. I dashed from the woods, and the crack of his gun echoed moments before the dirt exploded right at my feet. He hadn't missed—he was toying with me. I zigzagged, tried to keep moving, as my stepfather repeatedly shot the dirt inches from my feet. He wasn't going to let me make it to the shelter, and there was no way I could flee back to the woods.

I stopped. Stood in the field, bow in hand, and glared up at my stepfather. He stood defiantly on the rooftop. His rifle aimed directly at me. A red dot from his sight no doubt rested on my forehead. He backed away from the scope—he didn't need it—so his one good eye met my two.

"When a lion takes over a pride, he kills the lioness's cubs!" Every word was heavy, dripping with his hatred for me. "The cub does not kill the pride!"

Most likely for the last time, I wished that I could save my mother and half sister. *I must save them!* I had no doubt what would happen to them. Without his two sons—without his pride—my stepfather would start his colony again. Harsher. More violent. Stronger.

Nothing left to lose. I pulled my last arrow from the quiver. Nocked it. Ignored my stepfather's jeers as I did. But instead of drawing the string and shooting at him, I spun and crouched. A bullet passed through my hair. When I faced the woods, I shot my last arrow at one of the soldiers—aiming for and hitting him in the kneecap.

Bullets fired from the woods as soldiers fought back. My stepfather fired at them, ignoring me below. He could deal with me anytime.

The field between the woods and the house had become a war zone. I dashed for the cellar. When I reached it, I slammed the doors shut, though I knew they'd lock and my mother and half sister might still be prisoners in the house.

As for my stepfather's sons—I still couldn't wipe their bloodstains from my hands.

CHAPTER TWO

After thirty days in the shelter, I had a hard time breathing sometimes. I was too weak to fight. Too filled with fear. Something hard banged the other side of the door, and I jumped back. I grabbed my Glock and waited in case someone barged inside. The door was made of thick, reinforced steel. The jamb was also steel. *The walls are three feet of thick concrete*, I wrote in my notebook using a series of dashes and dots as I whispered the words over and over.

Another bang, but this one not from the outside. It couldn't have been. This noise was in my head, a sound I convinced myself I'd heard. I tucked the notebook into my back pocket.

Staggering to my feet, I tested the handle, and then paced back to the cot. I immediately returned to check the lock again while running my hands over my long, matted hair. *I'm locked in. If he's there, my stepfather is locked out* was my mantra as I continued to pace.

There's no choice! I have to leave my shelter, I told myself forcefully, loudly, in hopes I would believe it. *I must believe it!*

I'd already stayed so long that an unbearable stench had

seeped into the taste of the military rations I was eating. The once plentiful water was now down to a few liters. My choices were simple: risk my life on the other side of this door, or stay in my bunker until it becomes my coffin.

The lock snapped, and I jumped. Placing my palms on the door, I shoved, but it didn't budge. Was I that weak? I braced my shoulder against it and heaved with a grunt. Once in motion, it slid easily with a loud creak as if moaning. When it flew open completely, I stumbled into the secondary shelter.

I scrambled to my feet, and my eyes darted around. My only source of light, a lantern sitting in the bunker, was so low on oil that it cast dark shadows in the corners of the room. But it gave off enough light for me to see I was safe.

The cellar doors were also made of steel, and they were still locked—shut from the inside. I dusted myself off. Anything could be waiting outside. My stepfather. The soldiers. At least two months' worth of canned food and necessities lined the shelves. I didn't have to leave.

Cocking the gun, I stepped up to the cellar door. From inside the shelter, my home appeared undamaged. If the soldiers had won, wouldn't they have blown the house door from its hinges? Shot out the windows? If my stepfather had won, wouldn't *he* have, in order to get to me? I started to worry the soldiers I'd brought to my stepfather were less than successful. *Calm down*, I told myself. *He must be dead.*

I turned the wheel of the lock, and the gears clicked like a bank safe. When the wheel wouldn't crank anymore, the door unlocked. Anyone on the other side would know I was coming out. *Please, let the war be over.* I grabbed the door handle, and the cold metal tingled against my palms.

Children of Ruin

The door lifted more heavily than I'd remembered, and I found myself concentrating on it rather than on who might await me. When it slammed open, I immediately held up the gun and jumped back. My hands were shaking, and I turned back into the same scared boy I had promised myself never to be again.

Eventually, I lowered my Glock, climbed back up the stairs, and looked outside. I was right that the house was intact. The bright blue sky made me squint. Lush, green-leafed trees filled the woods facing the cellar. The grass was long and yellow. Throughout the yard were small piles of charred pages, their ashes floating on the wind. I caught one and, though its edges were burnt, I could still read a panel where Batman was holding the dead body of the second Robin, Jason Todd.

I lifted my foot over the lip of the doorframe. A piece of me enjoyed the moist grass that tickled my toes, and I wondered how long my feet had been naked. With each step, I felt as if the earth was pulling me back to the ground. I tried not to look at the sky. It was so high it might suck me into it at any moment. Something brushed against me, and I froze. *The wind. That's the wind.* Thirty days was a long time to be without the sky and fresh air. Both felt strange now.

When I rounded the house to the other side, I saw our shed. I heard in my head my stepfather's words to my mom—*You coddle the boy too much*—just before he'd drag me in there. Words he'd repeat until she stopped fighting him. Stopped protecting me. I'd scream as worries filled my head so much, so heavily, that I thought they might explode out my ears.

The shed was padlocked, but fear filled me so much

that I couldn't go near it. I left that place locked. Untouched.

All the windows in the house were locked tight with security bars, except the kitchen window. I wondered why it wasn't closed. *I could run and jump to the sill, pull myself inside.* But I couldn't have done that and protected myself if my stepfather were waiting for me in there. Was it a trap? I took a step, and the ground shook beneath me. No. My legs were shaking from a fear my body recognized, but my brain did not. I watched the windows for shadows but saw shadows everywhere. My senses were on fire—the sun scorched my skin, the wind burned my eyes, and the pollen singed my nose.

I couldn't say where my strength had come from, but suddenly I was running and leaping in the air for the sill. I imagined myself floating upward as if I would never stop.

I just made it, so I pulled myself up and inside. As I rolled over the sink, I held onto my gun. On the floor, I kicked out. Pushed myself against the counter. Saw nothing but shadows.

My heart beat so loudly I couldn't imagine hearing anything else. From the kitchen, I saw into the living room on the left, and down the hallway that led to the front door and bedrooms on the right. So far, I was alone. Alone. My breathing rasped. I made unfamiliar sounds. I felt as if the sky were about to fall, as if the whole house might be sucked up off the Earth. Something wet streamed down my cheeks. I wiped it away so I could see. Tears.

I stood on shaking legs, holding the gun out in front of me. I started down the hallway, but the farther I got into the house, the less sunlight was filtered through the shades. My parents' bedroom door was slightly ajar, and I peered inside the room. The master bed was a mess of sheets and blood. The dresser drawers lay broken on the floor—whatever had been in them was gone. I took out my notebook and I wrote, *Open window, empty house. Bloodstained sheets.* This might be important information later.

After I had written the words "bloodstained sheets," I couldn't help but grab the sheets and hold them to my cheeks. Beneath the stench of death was the scent of my mother—and I knew she was gone. I wrapped myself in the sheets, imagining the warmth was from her. I wished I could feel angry or sad. When she married my stepfather, she told me it was to protect me. Something about the debt my real dad had left us, her failure at getting a job, and how much she couldn't be alone. "He loves his two sons so much. You'll see," she had assured me. She was right. He loved his two sons.

The barrel of the Glock felt cold when I held it to my forehead. After dropping the sheet to the floor, I headed toward the room Kyle shared with Zeke. With each step I winced, thinking back on the times they pounded me with their fists. *They aren't in there. They can never hurt me again.* I pressed my ear against the closed door. Nothing. Then an odd rushing sound, like water going over a cliff. *Just the noise in my head.* Grasping the door handle, I twisted it. When the lock clicked, I stopped. I gave the door a push. It creaked open. I peered inside. The room was empty, save for a bunk bed tucked in one corner by a window and my cot in the far corner. There were no blankets. Someone had been there, but I was alone now.

In the living room was a ladder leading to the roof. I climbed it, emerging onto a roost—a flattened area. I could see the yard clearly, all the way to the edge of the surrounding woods and the one road that led in and out of our compound. I stepped on something hard that rolled, and when I looked down, I saw shell casings from an AK-47 but no gun.

I picked up a shell. It was cold. I spun in a circle, studying what was around me. The garden. My sister's swing. And bodies. About two dozen bodies rotting on the field, which explained the shells.

My stepfather must be alive. I wondered where he was now. Was he coming back? The silence suddenly fell over me, its weight nearly toppling me to the floor.

"Why did you leave the compound? Why were you not waiting to kill me?" I whispered.

It was time to leave the safety of the roost and wander the property. None of the house windows were broken, but bullet casings littered the outside walls. I took my steps slowly, each footstep bringing me closer to one of the dead soldiers. The buzzing of flies drummed in my ears. Every time the wind rushed, it brought with it a stench that made me gag. Maggots had eaten one soldier's flesh to the bone, and his bloated chest pushed out the seams of his flak jacket.

Flak jacket. Most striking was that he had one bullet hole in him—to the brain. I fell to my knees, engulfed in sunburned grass, and remembered the speech my stepfather gave before every meal. I flipped through my notebook and found where I had written that down.

We are living in end times, and there will be no god who raptures the likes of us into Heaven. We will be among the armies of the Earth, fighting for the remaining scraps.

My stepfather placed scraps on my plate. I had watched

with envy as his sons ate twice as much as me, and in pity as my mother and sister nibbled on even less. My stepfather feasted on the lion's share. When I was younger, I fantasized about how I could rise through the ranks. I imagined myself sitting side by side with my stepsiblings. I had vowed one day to become a part of the great army my stepfather had so often spoken of. And then my plate would also be full.

Now the end was here. And the army was one. Me. It was time to defend what was mine, even if there was nothing left to fill my plate but the rotting corpses before me.

Inside the secondary shelter, I counted two to three months' worth of food cans lining the wooden shelves. I twisted a can of mystery meat, and the shelves and wall popped out as one large unit. The unit slid to the right, revealing weapons. Funny how my stepfather felt they were more valuable to keep secret than the food.

I took out my notebook and wrote down the inventory. I had to record all of this: Three M16s, three Glock 30s, and three .22 rifles. Also three machetes, three hunting bows, dozens of arrows, and three slingshots. In non-weaponry, three of each: sleeping bags, night vision goggles, pepper spray cans, telescopic batons, and survival kits with the essentials (twenty waterproof matches, two candles, two flint sticks, one magnifying glass, and a compass). What hit home was that everything was in threes—for my stepfather and his two sons. It must have angered my stepfather no end that I had locked him out of the shelter and this treasure trove.

I slipped my notebook into my back pocket before grabbing two machetes from the wall. Their weight was perfectly balanced, and I swung them in an upward arch from left to right. Not some amateur hack-and-slash I'd learned from watching *Friday the 13th*, but a practiced swing trained into me since the day of my stepfather's accident. I found a double scabbard with a crisscrossed strap for the back, and put that on. I sheathed the two machetes. On my belt, I wore the telescopic baton like a sword.

Tonight I would sleep in the roost, out in the open for the first time in weeks. I filled a backpack with night vision goggles, some bagged military rations—Meals Ready to Eat, or MREs, bags filled with a pouch of stew, crackers, peanut butter, a chocolate bar and gum—and, just for safety, a slingshot. I also grabbed a rifle. Finally, I took a sleeping bag and a handful of *Batman* comics.

The sun was now well past its peak in the sky. Darkness was falling fast. With the night vision goggles, I'd be able to see if anyone was coming around in the dark. Before returning to the house, I drew my machetes and held them in front of me. I had to be ready for anything. But was I ready to kill? I thought about my stepfather's sons, and how long it had taken to wipe their blood from my hands. *That wasn't in cold blood*, I told myself. *That was different. I am not a murderer.* Crows cawed, sounding like "Bury dead! Bury dead!" For now I ignored the dead—the living were more dangerous. If people were watching, if my stepfather were waiting, they'd be hiding in the woods.

What if this had been just an ordinary day and I'd been getting ready for school? My two stepsiblings would have taunted me for having to go to public school while they stayed home. "You are the eyes and ears for all of us," my stepfather would tell me as a warning, so I wouldn't forget my duty was to *not* make friends nor do well in classes. It made him angry that I had excelled in English, since that made the teachers notice me.

"Hide your intelligence," he had instructed me. What made him happiest was when everyone called me the "weird kid." When I was "invisible" to the other students, someone they would have the most intimate discussions around without even caring if I had overheard. My friends were my favorite novels, in which I'd discovered people I could relate to, such as Ralph in *Lord of the Flies* or Peter in *Cue for Treason* or Peeta in *The Hunger Games*. All unlikely heroes, all boys I wanted to be just like.

Each time I learned something new—what each family did for a living, who was building pools or buying cabins or leasing speedboats—I made notes in my little journal. I'd also discovered who had fallout shelters, though most were just remnants of the Cold War era.

Once in the roost, I rested my bag at my feet. The sun was nearly down, and the night was coming fast. I closed my eyes, drinking deeply of the crisp night air. My stepfather would have scolded me if he were here. *You have no plan.*

"I *had* a plan," I mumbled out loud, "but it doesn't look like the soldiers killed you."

A military meal helped stave off hunger, and a sleeping bag draped over my shoulders held the cold at bay. I'd replaced the stone ceiling I had watched for the last thirty days with stars. I made a mark in my notebook for every star I counted. Before the world fell, my mother spent her nights telling me, "You're weak and can't protect me." Not long after she'd married my stepfather, she offered no more hugs goodnight, no bedtime kisses on my forehead. She spent her attention on my crying sister.

Curiously, my sister cried a lot. She was the only one born both of my mother and stepsiblings' father. Surely, she was his favorite—she was the only one he visited each evening.

Howling wolves snapped me from my memory. The pack spoke to one another as they hunted, their calls surrounding me. Crickets, frogs, even the wind bristling against leaves pushed heavily on me. Inside my shelter was silence, my beating heart the only noise. Out there on the roof, I was deafened by memories.

I couldn't stay awake all night. My mental strength would wither without proper care of myself. I lay back against the surrounding wall and forced myself to look at the stars. As the wolves howled louder, I howled back at them. Silence. Then the wolves called back to me, and I was no longer alone.

CHAPTER THREE

I discovered I'd fallen asleep when a piercing scream jerked me awake. The world was a deep blue, except against the horizon peeking through the trees, where the sun glowed orange and yellow. Again, a shriek. The loudest noise in thirty days. My hand instinctively grasped my machete, but from where I sat, the better weapon was the slingshot or rifle. Another scream. This time I recognized the sound. A girl, helpless for sure.

When the screaming turned constant, it became a voice turned into a weapon. A hope that someone would hear and come to the rescue. A chance that the noise would scare off an aggressor. At times I had drawn that weapon, useless as it was.

I peered through binoculars and scanned the woods. At first, nothing. Then I spied a skirmish in a clearing just a hundred yards away. *Weird.* A group of men were dragging a girl toward my home. Three men to be exact. None of them were my stepfather.

One held the girl by her wrists. The other two were so close to the girl that if I'd tried to take them out with the rifle, I could have easily have hit her. She was fully clothed and trying to bite them. One of the men wiped his face as though she had spit on him when she stopped screaming.

The one who had just wiped his face shouted, and I could hear him clearly. Not words. Just a voice. He seemed to be shouting at Machete Man, who gripped the knife as if an invisible barrier existed between him and the girl. I considered trying to help her, but that would have exposed me. My stepfather was cunning at setting traps like this.

The girl stared at the man holding her, but he ignored her. Her trembling lips moved fast—she was begging for her life, no doubt. Most striking was the bloodstain on her right shoulder. She was hurt. And I recognized her from school. Kady. Kady Tremblay. I knew everything about her family. Hers was the only family I hadn't reported to my stepfather. I owed her. A month into the school year a group of boys—all her friends—had decided to make an example of the "weird kid." Tom, the football hero, was the leader and the one who had made a big scene of it. They took me out back of the school to beat me up, all four of them. The first punch was the hardest to take. I wanted to fight back. I could have killed them—which was why I *didn't* fight back. My stepfather didn't want me training to fight, and he didn't know how much I had learned by listening and watching. I practiced in secret when everyone else was asleep. The weaker he thought I was, the stronger I'd be when the world fell.

After the fight, I discovered that Kady had heard about her buddies' plans. That was why she'd run out—she wanted to stop them. Yet when the small crowd of kids stood around cheering, she had acted no differently than any of them. But afterward, when they'd all gone home, she came back to see if I was okay. She even took me to her house and patched me up. That's when I had learned about her fallout shelter. Hers was the only shelter I never added to my stepfather's map. My thank-you gift to her.

I lowered the binoculars. Did I want to get involved? My training told me no. Kady was just a casualty. Hundreds of "Kadys" probably shared her fate. The memory of her soft fingers on my wounded face made me reconsider. I donned the rucksack and strapped on my machetes. I scrambled down the ladder to the living room. Slipped out the front door. And as I ran to the clearing, I drew the machetes. But was I ready to kill? No. They were just creeps. I put away the machetes and drew my baton. A quick flick and the telescopic rod extended a full three feet.

Another scream.

I ran faster.

I entered the clearing. Held my chin up. I wanted to look confident, like someone who could easily take out these men. Inside my head, I had doubts. Three of them. Bigger than me. Two held menacing weapons—more dangerous than the baton I had in my hand. In the center of the clearing in the woods, a strong, burly, bearded man twisted Kady's hand behind her back. Kady was on her knees, hunched over the grass with her head facing down. The skinny man with the machete held his weapon above his head. He gripped the knife as though his training was from too many horror movies. His technique was all wrong, the angle easy to block or dodge. The third man, short and pudgy, stood off to the side a little, holding a shotgun.

"Do it! Stab her stomach!" the bearded man yelled. He must have been yelling that all along. Probably because he knew if the skinny man didn't do it, he'd have to.

Skinny Man shook his head, his eyes moist, on the

brink of tears. The one with the shotgun just looked away. Had they caught her trying to scavenge from them and were preserving their survival by killing any potential competition? It's what my stepfather would have done.

"Stay back!" the bearded man shouted when he saw me, his voice shrill.

"Ethan!" Kady screamed. Hearing my name spoken out loud after silence for so long made me pause. When I faltered, she sobbed, "Help me! Please!"

The bearded man turned and raised his backhand to slap her. I moved in. Hit him hard behind the knee with the baton. He keeled over. I swiped into his chest with my fist and reset into a fighting stance. Staggered my feet. Held my baton like a sword. The other two men didn't move.

Breathing heavily, the bearded man said, "Get him!"

Shotgun Man pointed his weapon at me. His hands shook, and he closed his eyes. He had as much chance of hitting his companions as he did me. I rushed forward, bringing the baton down on the muzzle, forcing it to the ground. He fired, and mud and gravel sprayed everywhere. My backfist slammed across his face. He toppled to the ground, landing hard on his back.

The men stared at me and then at each other. Each of them seemed hopeful the other would take me down, but none was brave enough to do it. My blood was on fire with adrenaline. My eyes were wide and must have looked crazy. My teeth gritted as I snarled. I must have looked like a wild animal. I had to end this now, or take a chance and flee. Was I a lion, or was I a mouse?

Before I acted, Kady clawed the man holding her across his face. He let her go, keeling over with a yelp.

Children of Ruin

Kady grabbed my hand and we dashed into the woods. At first we headed in the direction I had come from, toward my shelter, but when the adrenaline rush ended, I thought more clearly. I needed to know what supplies she had, without her knowing what I had. I changed direction toward her home.

"Where are you taking me?" Kady whimpered as she pulled free from my grip. She rubbed her wrist where I had left a red mark.

"Home. Your home," I said in a calm voice.

She seemed to digest this as we stood in the woods awhile. With a nod, she started walking. I wanted to know who those men were, and why they wanted to kill her. But her pained expression told me she wasn't yet ready to talk. Nor was I, as I realized fully that the world had finally become a place without the old rules. A place where everything I had been taught finally made sense.

CHAPTER FOUR

As we climbed down the ladder into Kady's underground bunker, she stopped weeping. At the bottom of the ladder, a six-foot-long hallway faced us. Kady walked into the darkness, and I stayed at the ladder where a little light shone down. I squinted but couldn't see all the way inside. She hadn't ignited any lamps, but I smelled something strong. Not burning lamp oil. Not even the same humid, putrid stench like that in my shelter. A floral scent like the one my mom always brought into the house. Had my mom made it to my shelter, it probably would have wound up with that scent as well.

"Your clothes, I ca—" Kady started to say. She stopped and swallowed hard.

I walked up to her and, as my eyes adjusted to the darkness, saw her hands were shaking. Was she afraid of those men, or was it me she now feared?

"Thanks," she mumbled, as if knowing my thoughts. "They were going to k—"

Her voice cut off and she leaned against the wall. Her hand covered her mouth, and tears emerged in her eyes again. I wanted to comfort her, but I just didn't know how.

"I have food," I said, as if that fixed everything. What I

wanted to say was, *No one followed us. You're safe.*

"Give me your clothes. I can wash them," Kady told me, a steadiness now to her tone. I watched her body posture soften.

"How are you going to wash them?" As I imagined an old washing board, Kady flicked a switch. A soft hum sounded and lights came up.

"Electricity," she said as she walked farther inside.

I kicked off my shoes and entered what looked like an underground house three times the size of my shelter, with a living room and a kitchen separated by a pass-through. I spied a couch and coffee table facing a big-screen TV.

"Don't even think about sitting on anything until you shower. You can wear one of my dad's robes until your clothes are clean."

"How are you powering all this stuff?" I asked, almost speechless that even after the Fall there were still the haves and have-nots.

"A generator. When the batteries run low, it kicks in."

Bet that's how the men found you. I took mental note. A generator creates exhaust, which would have clued in anyone happening by. As I started piecing all this together, Kady extended her arms to me. I backed up a little, unsure what she wanted.

"Your jacket. You can toss your other clothes into the hallway when you're in the bathroom. It's the first door on the right."

I slipped off my machetes and coat and handed her only the coat.

"We're going to have to talk about who those men were." My voice was grainy and low, a little rusty from not being used in so long. I had this urge to say, "I am

Batman," but doubted she would have found it funny.

She nodded and carefully took my coat without upsetting any of the dirt from it.

I went to the bathroom where I could learn if she'd been alone. Beside the sink, I found one toothbrush. Inside a closet were towels and boxes of "girl stuff." I assumed Kady had a storage room somewhere with more. My stepfather had never planned to take my mom with him into the shelter when the end came—I knew this because he hadn't stockpiled anything for her.

I quickly wrote down everything I saw: *Two towels, one bath and one face. Make-up.* (I didn't know what any of it was, so I just wrote "make-up.") *Toothpaste, one toothbrush, and mouthwash.* Lastly, I found a curler and a blow dryer, and recorded these items, too. I reasonably assumed she'd been the only one using the shelter.

As I put the notebook into my pocket, I wondered where the water was coming from. I noticed a small septic tank beneath the toilet.

Kady banged on the door, interrupting my observations.

"Don't flush too much toilet paper down the toilet! The septic tank will clog, and then I'm screwed!" After a brief silence, she then asked, "Are you done taking off your clothes yet?"

I removed my clothes and passed them through the door so only my arm showed. When she took the clothes, I retrieved my arm and realized my notebook was in my jeans pocket. I'd have to remember anything else I found, instead of writing it down. The shower started automatically when I climbed into it. The warm water was completely invigorating as it washed the sweat and grime off me. I just couldn't believe how decadent this place was, and could only guess that her parents really had no concept of what the end of the world was going to be like.

Had those men wanted her shelter?

After I had toweled off, I took a good look at myself in the mirror, surprised at how much muscle I had lost. My living off MREs with very little exercise for four weeks had taken its toll. Still, I had a solid frame and I was quick. What I needed most was more exercise.

"You about done?" she asked, after rapping on the door outside.

"I need the robe," I said, trying to sound tough to hide my embarrassment at being naked.

She laughed, and at first that made me mad. Did she do that to purposely make me feel stupid?

"Just use a towel. I have the robe for you out here. I won't peek, promise," she said in a way that made me feel as if we were back in high school.

After wrapping a towel around my waist, I grabbed my machetes. When I opened the door, more smells wafted up my nose. It smelled like food, and I wondered what rations she'd been living off. If she had a grid, she must have had a fridge. I needed to write this down.

Around the corner in the living room, I took a seat on the couch. I watched her through the pass-through, cooking at a stove. That's when I noticed—she was clean. I mean, *clean*. Her hair was combed straight, except where it curled halfway down her back. Her nails were long and painted, and she'd redone her makeup.

"You're staring," she said with a curled upper lip. She

tossed my notebook to me through the pass-through. "What's with all the dots and dashes?"

I wondered how much she had gleaned from it, and if that made her a problem for me. "That's how I take notes. One day all this will be important."

"With dots and dashes? Riiiiight. How did you survive?" she asked, rolling her eyes. Then, with a kinder voice said, "I mean, I'm glad and all, but how?"

My stepfather trained me to never give away information. Kady's shelter may have been a palace, but when the generator ran out of gas, it would be a death trap. Clean air required vents. My guess was that any air vents in here were run off electricity. Mine were, too, but electricity from the hand-pump generators that I wound every day. Cranking them was probably the only thing that kept me from completely wasting away.

"Are you alone? Where's your family?" I asked, knowing I needed to be in charge of questions. I discreetly wrote *one generator*.

She lifted the lid off the pot and stirred whatever was inside. It smelled good. She grabbed a ladle and filled two bowls. Two utensils. One to stir and one to scoop. She'd also made enough for leftovers. She hadn't changed her ways since the end had come.

"I don't know. No one was home when the emergency broadcast came. Remember when I was the one protecting you?" Her words trailed off with a quiet snort, and I wondered if she wished the world still worked that way.

She placed a bowl before me on the coffee table and rested the other on her lap. She sat beside me. Tears occasionally fell from her eyes, and I could see she struggled to maintain her composure. I probably should have reached out and touched her shoulder. Comforted her. Isn't that what a person did in times like this?

"I guess we're even. I'm also alone," I told her, remembering my mom once telling me that shared experiences were a good way to build trust.

"Were your parents in the city, too?" she asked, knowing my family never left the colony. We were all known as that weird cult that kept to itself.

"How much fuel do you have left for your generator?" I asked, trying to stay in charge.

"I have extra gas drums." She paused. "Where did you learn to fight like that?"

A memory of that day when we were sitting in her kitchen as she bandaged me up flashed. She probably felt sorry for me because I was small, which in her mind meant I was defenseless. Back then I counted on presumptions like that to survive school unnoticed.

I ignored her question and focused on the bowl in front of me. Brown gravy, chunks of beef and potato, green beans, peas, and carrots. Smelled like stew; could have been dog food. Either way, it was nutrition. Kady scooped a spoonful into her mouth, and I waited for her to swallow. Since she'd used the same ladle for both our bowls, she couldn't have had the opportunity to poison mine. Not that I really believed she would have, but I had to be careful.

As I ate a mouthful, the heat swarmed my body. For the first time, I realized I was cold and shivering.

"What happened to the world?" I asked.

She stared at me with her head tilted slightly. "You really have no idea, do you?"

"The government sent soldiers to arrest my

stepfather." Not exactly the truth, but as close as I wanted to tell her. "I fled to the shelter. When I came back out, everyone was gone."

"There was an outbreak of the sickness in the town, and the CDC brought in soldiers to contain it," she whispered and looked away. "You do know about the sickness, right?"

"We heard rumors. Radio reports." My stepfather had disseminated information and chose to interpret much of what was happening.

"Started out as the flu. Then, an outbreak of rabies. People were urged to stay at home, but people got cabin fever and went to work, the grocery store, and the movies anyway." Kady's hands shook as she ate her meal. She was shell-shocked, and I shouldn't push. At least not now.

"Have you checked your house?" I asked.

She shook her head, and I sensed fear in her eyes. I could have imagined it, but there seemed more to her story than what she'd told me. It made me think back to those men, and I wondered if they might be waiting for us outside in greater numbers. They would most certainly return better prepared. This shelter, while a luxury, was also a target. We couldn't fortify it, and even if we had cameras set up in the yard, we couldn't man them all the time with only two of us.

"You can wear my brother's clothes until yours are dry." Her voice turned soft. "And you might as well keep his clothes. I doubt he's still alive."

I nodded. I wanted to press my questions and get answers from her, but I'd get more if I built trust. I wandered over to the sleeping quarters where I counted one double bed tucked into a corner and one bunk bed tucked into the other. I also counted two wardrobes, and noted all of this in my notebook. I wondered how the rest of her family had died.

My hands were still shaking as I stood in front of the wardrobe by the bunk beds. A part of me wanted to curl up on the bed and lie there forever. When I read the Narnia books, they made me feel like a boy living in the wrong world. Now, I needed to feel the way Peter felt in *The Lion, the Witch and the Wardrobe*. As if this were the greatest adventure ever—as if I had finally been sent home.

But in my mind, I heard my stepfather's words, reminding me that in the end, we would be turned into kings. *Kings do not feel fear.*

The wardrobe's doors opened easily. Kady's clothes were on one side, and her brother's were pushed tightly to the opposite corner. He had dressed in jeans that were too big for him and long shirts with skateboard logos.

Unlike Peter, when *I* walked through the wardrobe, I would do so looking like a tool.

I put on a pair of sweat pants and a shirt that went just below my ass. I tied the pants tight and cut the legs so they could hang better. The shoulder straps for my machetes held the shirt tight. I threw the rucksack over one shoulder.

The mirror was hung by french cleats and sat a little loosely on the inside door. Catching a glimpse of myself, I chuckled at how ridiculous I looked. I pushed the mirror along the hooks. It slid out completely. *This just might save my life.*

When I left the bedroom, Kady was glancing at me with her lips curled in a smile. But spying the mirror, she stormed in front of me. Blocked my way to the hatch.

"Where do you think you're going with that?"

With my shoulder, I pushed her aside, leaning the mirror gently against the wall at the bottom of the ladder. I considered the best way to use the mirror to see if anyone were waiting for me outside. Kady kept yelling that the mirror was important, and was asking how she was supposed to do her hair if I broke it. As I tried to ignore her, I couldn't help but wonder if she really understood the old world wasn't coming back. I couldn't climb the ladder and hold the mirror. If I asked Kady to pass it to me, she'd just put it back.

My mom used to do this thing when she wanted my stepfather to do something he refused to do. She'd put her hand on the back of his head and look directly in his eyes. Her voice would turn soft, and she'd hold his gaze until he gave in. It was worth a shot.

I stood in front of Kady and placed my hand on the back of her head, but she flinched a little. My stepfather had never done that, and I wondered if I was doing it right. I stared into her eyes. In a low voice I said, "If those men are waiting for me outside, I have a chance of seeing them in the mirror. If they kill me, there's nothing stopping them from killing you."

Kady's eyes widened. I wondered if she understood. I wasn't sure how long I should stand there with my hand on her, so I awkwardly took it away. I gave her the mirror and started up the ladder. When I saw that she wasn't leaving to return the mirror to her room, I climbed the rest of the ladder and gently opened the hatch just enough to peek outside.

Sunlight poured inside, blinding me with spots. I

reached down for the mirror, and Kady handed it up to me. Ignoring my sun blindness, I threw open the hatch and lifted out the mirror. The area looked clear. Green fields, a big house. No gardens, no chicken coops. *What was she planning to live on?* I wondered as I handed Kady back the mirror.

"Do we have a plan?" her voice cracked and shook as if with fear.

She's wondering if I'm coming back.

It had crossed my mind that once I was away, I should stay away. But if I did that, I would no doubt sentence Kady to death. I might as well have left her to the mercy of those men. No matter what, I was now responsible for her.

"Information," I said flatly. "I'm going into town to see what exactly we're dealing with."

"How long will you be?"

I shrugged, as if that were an answer. Of course what she really wanted to know was how long should she wait before she started to worry? She was going to run out of power and food here, and if I didn't come back, this fancy shelter would eventually be a fancy tomb. For her sake, if not my own, I would have to survive.

"People have changed," she said, as though speaking to someone who didn't understand English. "The sickness made them . . . different."

"What's waiting for us out there?"

She shrugged, but I couldn't tell if it was from not knowing or not wanting to tell me. Either way, we had an understanding. She had no option but to trust me.

As I emerged from the hatch, I drew a machete.

"You can use the bike," Kady called up. "It's in the

shed, in back of the house."

I ignored her as my eyes adjusted to the light. There could be guns pointed right at me—though I had my doubts those men would have returned just yet. If they weren't ready to kill, then they weren't desperate enough and must have still had supplies.

The red sky on the horizon made me realize I'd never actually just looked at a sunrise. I stood still as I smelled a sweet-smelling breeze. I listened to the rustle of leaves each time the breeze rose. Without really knowing why, I wondered if my stepfather would be proud of how I had survived.

"Your job is to not get caught," I recalled my stepfather telling me once when I was just seven years old. He had decked me out in camo and armed me with a kali stick—a three-foot bamboo rod used in martial-arts training.

We had been standing at the edge of the woods, enacting what would be the first of many times this scene would play out. I thought he was taking me on my first hunting trip, and I was so excited that he had finally included me.

"Samuel, he's just a boy," my mother had pleaded as a way to keep me from going. When he slapped her for it, I had felt some satisfaction. After all, being treated like a child was what kept me from advancing in the ranks.

Mornings like this, I usually spent rushing through the woods, trying to go in as deep as I could. I would have a fifteen-minute head start, and then Kyle and Zeke would be sent in after me. The first time seemed like a game of hide-and-seek—but little did I know what would happen when they found me.

Children of Ruin

I forced the memory to stop there. I refused to recall any more. Especially how much I would come to regret not being the kind of son who protected his mother. I refocused on my task. *Survive.* I kept my machetes drawn and my eyes peeled. Kady's house was larger than most in the area, and her parents were richer because they weren't farmers but scientists.

For a moment, I considered that there might be notes inside the house. Her dad might have left clues as to what had happened to the world around us. I would have to explore it when I got back.

Behind the house, I found the shed. Most farms in the area would have had wooden sheds made generations before, but this one was aluminum with what looked like an unbreakable padlock.

I gave the lock a tug, just out of frustration, and it popped open. Made sense it wasn't scrambled since we lived in the middle of nowhere. Didn't make sense they had it, unless there was a plan in place to hide something valuable in there. I imagined a scenario where the men forced Kady to unlock the shed before taking her into the woods to kill her. If my stepfather had kidnapped her, it's what he would have done.

Slowly, I opened the door. But all I found inside was an Xmotos XB-21D dirt bike. Even though I didn't have my driver's license, riding dirt bikes in the country was a rite of passage. This was no different in my family, except that for us, it was for survival, not recreation.

In my notebook, I wrote what I found: *three sets of helmets and four sets of Sixsixone Rage pressure suit bike armor— one large, two mediums, and a small.* I assumed these were for Kady, her parents, and her brother. The whole family was taken care of. The armor strapped on the back but protected the chest, shoulders and stomach. I felt a little like Goldilocks choosing between the big, medium and small size. Unlike for Goldilocks, the medium fit me best and was slim enough to wear under my jacket. I should have worn the helmet, but I worried about it limiting my vision. That could have meant the difference between living and dying.

The bike was only half filled with fuel, and there were no gas canisters inside the shed. Kady had said there were extras, but I thought it might be better to find fuel in town and preserve what was here. Electricity was more important than the bike. If I couldn't find gasoline in town, I probably could at one of the farms along the way. Either way, walking home would be better than having no generator.

Pulling the bike out of the shed, I decided to walk it out of the area for an hour before starting it so the noise wouldn't alert the men that we'd returned.

CHAPTER FIVE

I'm getting back in shape, I told myself as I came to a stop where the dirt ended and the tarred road began. A dark shadow crossed the road where the trees filtered the sun from the path. From that point, the sun shone freely. Loon Lake Road was behind me, with pines and poplars spotting the hills on either side. All those great places where I could run and hide were what I was leaving. An open highway that led north to Clinton and south to Cache Creek was ahead of me.

Showered in the sunlight, I stood still, enjoying the heat as it prickled my skin. An odd sensation I hadn't felt in thirty days. I kicked the bike starter, but nothing happened. I tried again, and the motor sputtered. My legs were sore and my heart pounded from the long walk. I had to try again. With a grunt, I gave it a good kick, and the engine roared to life. Gray smoke burst from it before it ran clean. I hoped the sound would lead anyone nearby toward me and away from Kady.

I pointed the bike north and sped along the twisting highway. I had to weave back and forth to avoid potholes. An end to government was an end to services. No more roadwork after the winter months.

As I rode the bike, warm air blew from the rolling brown hills, brushing my face and hair. Without electricity, much of the farmland had dried up from no irrigation. Along the way, I found many boarded-up roadside stops, and the houses, ones that had looked abandoned even before the Fall, now reminded me I'd have no shortage of junk to scavenge. Long before the apocalypse, the North had been closing up fast with the end of pulp mills.

My thoughts drifted to Kady, and what I'd done by rescuing her. We could pool together our stuff, so it wasn't as if she'd be sponging off me. Having another voice to hear besides my own would help my chances of survival— even if she just kept me from going crazy. But I was taking on a baby. A child. Someone who had spent her life learning cheers instead of survival. When she risked her popularity to bandage my wounds, she had proved to me that she wasn't vacuous and she didn't think first of herself. For now, if we were attacked, it wouldn't be two on my side—instead I'd be fighting for two. She'd rely on my ability to get water, hunt for food, and, when it became necessary, maybe even kill. Those men would be back. I could train her to be a warrior and a hunter like me.

Ahead I saw the gas station and, just beyond that, the historic frontier-style buildings. The silhouette of a body hanging from the canopy of the station stopped me from blazing down the highway. I left the bike running as I climbed off it. It could have been just someone who had committed suicide because they couldn't handle how the world had changed. Or it could have been that someone was trying to send a message—someone who was watching me right then.

Just to be safe, I drew my machetes.

Children of Ruin

Suddenly, I was aware of the crunch of stones beneath my feet as I listened for anyone inside the gas station. A wind I hadn't noticed before whistled in my ears, making it harder to hear anything. I took small, careful steps. I approached the glass door of the kiosk, which was slightly ajar, and ducked beneath an ice machine to stay covered from the window. Either someone was still inside, or they'd left in too much of a hurry to close the door properly.

The glass was so dusty and the station was so dark inside that peering through was nearly impossible. I could tell that the aisles had shelving so high several people could have been hiding there. Using the tip of my machete, I carefully pushed the door open. A bell dinged and sent me jumping back.

I waited to see if anyone stirred inside. When no one did, I stepped through the doorway.

My eyes adjusted quickly, and I recoiled from a stench like rotting meat. My guess was that, without electricity, whatever sandwiches were in the fridges had spoiled. I walked around to check the aisles. Empty. Nothing even on the shelves, except a layer of dust. No impressions left in the dust, so I knew the place had been stripped clean long before.

Others had scavenged anything of value here long before I arrived, so I headed back outside. The wind brushed the dirt from the road, dusting my boots. I imagined an old western, as though I were a drifter told to just pass on through. Reminded me of the book *Shane*— but I was far from a retired gunslinger. I hadn't wandered into the old western town looking for peace, but rather steeled for battle. I breathed deeply of this freedom and drew my second machete. Today had different rules.

Who was this man outside? The canopy that the rope was attached to creaked as he swayed in the breeze. Did he try to protect himself, or had fear seeped into his soul with no one left to save him?

"Were you looted first, or did they come after you killed yourse—?"

When the wind spun his body a little, I stopped talking. His head was twisted to the side, and his face turned toward me. He had a bullet hole through his left eye. Nothing around that he could have climbed on to get that high. Someone had killed him. Maybe they hanged him, and then couldn't watch him suffer, so they shot him. When his body had spun enough that his chest faced me, I saw a sign around his neck. It read, In the Land of the Blind.

"The One-Eyed Man is King," I whispered, finishing my stepfather's favorite quote. He said it so often, and with such vigor, that I could never forget it.

This wasn't summer break. I had an enemy. One who might have been close. I couldn't see any cluster of trees where I could camouflage the bike, so I propped it against the side of the gas station and hoped it looked abandoned. If I hid it out in the open, it might work as a quick getaway should I find myself not alone.

The road was still my best path, even though taking it might expose me more. But there could be traps in the fields, or worse, people waiting. What I needed to do was climb the first building along Cariboo Highway and see if I couldn't jump between roofs. I chuckled as I reminded myself the apocalypse hadn't turned me into Batman.

As I entered a strip of buildings, I refocused on what

was before me. North Road Trading Post was my best bet for supplies. Also, if anyone else were alive, chances were that would be where they'd holed up. I stepped carefully past abandoned cars and trucks, noting that most had broken windows and flat tires. None had been stripped. That could be good news for me. If they all still had gasoline, we could use Kady's generator for some time.

The quiet would have been more jarring if I had been from a big city. Small towns were always serene, which was why people stayed. And why they left. I felt safe for the first time walking these streets. The danger that might have been lurking in shadows was nothing compared to what once walked in the light. I recalled coming into the town one time after school, just to see what it was like. My stepfather forbade this. It would draw attention to my family.

Tom and his friends had found me again, and I was beaten up a second time, with no Kady there to stop Tom. Each time his fist hit my face or body, I wanted to fight back. But that would have brought his parents to my home, and everyone would have known that I knew how to defend myself. As angry as my stepfather was going to be when he found out I had traveled into town, he would be twice that knowing I knew how to fight back.

Across from the service station in an empty lot, a sign read LOTS FOR SALE. Wooden posts with shingles nailed all over them littered the lot, some standing as high as eight feet. I walked past the sign to the posts and read a few of the shingles. Names of people who had visited, including the name of someone from as far away as Kristiansand, Norway, along with an arrow pointing toward what I assumed must have been Norway.

Civilization once thrived here, and the world once visited to see what a historic frontier town was like. The lives of us who lived here—reduced to a theme park.

I noticed a shingle that read "Kelvin, I'm okay. Please find me," and another, "Status update: 'This sucks.'" It was a message board for people wanting to find friends and family. This was the new Internet.

A shadow appeared over the road and disappeared. I ducked close to the ground. Someone else was here—a girl dressed in camo, who ran into the auto shop. I didn't think she'd seen me, but I also couldn't take any chances. Maybe she was friendly, or maybe she was with my stepfather. I ran behind a truck and tried to peek around it. The garage doors to the shop were open, and the medium-sized girl was rummaging through the tools. She was clad in a tan tunic, trousers, and beret. She even wore a green necktie and belt. Sweat dripped down my armpits—but I didn't dare dress down from my bike armor, as it protected me. Since the girl was still wearing a uniform, she was under someone's command.

I stayed hidden. I watched to see if anyone else met with her. I heard a buzz, and she took a radio from her belt and answered. I couldn't hear what she said. Were they on their way? Had she found something of value? She reached for an AK-47 I hadn't seen resting against the tool chest. She bent down, hoisting what looked like a hockey bag over her shoulder. By the clanking, I guessed she must have filled it with tools.

"What's your twenty?" she called over her radio. Without waiting for an answer, she dropped her bag and radio and brought up her gun. She pointed it into the darkness, far into the garage where I couldn't see.

Children of Ruin

Whoever used to own the shop—Greg Something-or-other—was he still holed up in there? Was this army brat stealing supplies from someone who was still home?

"You alive?" the army brat shouted at the darkness. "I said: 'You alive?' I'm going to give you to the count of three, and then I shoot. One . . ."

If it was Greg inside the garage, and he was just protecting himself against being robbed, would I let this army brat kill him?

"Two . . ."

Or should I stay secret, hidden from view? This army brat had contacted someone. Was the government still active, or had someone else taken over?

"Three!"

She fired six times, and then she paused. Her stance looked practiced, and she didn't recoil the way someone would had they never shot a semi-automatic assault rifle. She was definitely the real deal. I had to assume that Greg was dead.

Army Brat stayed poised for a few more seconds before grabbing her hockey bag and slinging it over her shoulder. She started for the street, in the same direction as me. I crouched behind the truck. I didn't know if I could take her in a fight—she was army, so she'd had training. I definitely wouldn't be able to take her in a gunfight. No fooling myself about her, either. Army Brat had just killed.

I would have followed her to her camp if I had known she was alone. But she was on a radio, and since she was scavenging tools and not food, I assumed she was well prepared. I took out my notebook and wrote down everything I saw, including that she had taken the highway south toward Cache Creek. She was alert to her surroundings, talking on her radio. One day I would source her out.

Growling behind me. I'd been too focused on the army brat. I cranked my head slowly, and in the street a few paces behind me was a collie, just older than a pup. I stood still, tucked my notebook into my pocket, and tried to see anything odd about the dog. Kady had mentioned rabies, and in this world that would surely kill me. The collie's ears lay flat against her head, and her tail was tucked between her legs. She watched me from under her brow with her head lowered in submission. The tags on her collar jingled when she moved. I was impressed that she had survived. Smaller dogs than she had no doubt become food for coyotes, but ones that adapted to hunting for meals would do well in this new world.

Before I'd finished my thoughts, something heavy hit the metal hood of the truck beside me. A Rottweiler over 130 pounds slammed into me full on. I stumbled forward. Panic burned my veins. His jaw clamped on my shoulder. *Is he sick? Did he bite into my skin?* My weapons fell to the ground just before I did. I braced my palms flat on the dirt and pushed myself up. The armor protected me, and I elbowed the dog off me before he could get another bite.

The collie ran full force, her teeth bared and saliva dripping from her maw. I grabbed at my weapons.

The collie wasn't fighting me for territory; she was fighting me for survival. For these dogs, I was probably the closest thing to fresh meat they'd smelled out in weeks. That made them dangerous—and hard to predict. I didn't want them to bite my skin, to miss the armor. I hacked desperately with the machetes. If I went crazy, lost control,

Children of Ruin

I could possibly give them the edge they needed.

Stay calm, I could hear my stepfather say to me. Even though his voice wasn't real, I forced myself to obey.

Barks and yaps echoed against the buildings as more dogs gathered around me. I slashed with my machete and heard a squeal as I hit flesh. The Rott went down, and an equally big Doberman took his place. He growled with all teeth bared. With one alpha male dead, there'd be another waiting in line.

"You've been hoping for this day, haven't you?" I said to the dog, of its new place as alpha.

We circled one another like the wild beasts we'd become. I was the beast that had trespassed into someone else's territory. But this territory should be mine. It had to be mine, or I wouldn't survive. I was betting the dog had an equal stake in this fight. If he was going to take charge of the pack, he would have to prove his mettle.

"Okay, Dog, how long have you been waiting for something else to take him out?" I whispered low to the Doberman, in a way that sounded like a growl.

Dog growled back, lips curled to show me his bloodstained teeth. Had he killed recently, or was this a sign of rabies? I sliced the air in front of me with one of my machetes. Dog cringed and flinched. It understood that, though I didn't have teeth and claws, my hand could bite as hard.

A squeal from behind me, and Dog's shackles went up. His eyes grew wide with fear. I spun around. This is what I didn't want—to come here and be noticed. Greg had limped into the street, still wearing his oil-stained overalls. Army Brat must have missed, or maybe hit him in the leg. Boils covered his neck all the way up to one of his eyes.

Pus sprayed from some of the boils as he moved toward me.

A Staffordshire bull terrier jumped at him, but Greg bit it and threw it aside. I wondered if they were fighting over me as several dogs leaped in his way. Greg scratched or bit them before tossing them aside. Most of the pack scattered except for a small puppy. The puppy, also a Staffordshire bull terrier, barked at Greg, refusing to move. Greg lunged at it. Alpha Dog leaped between them. I gained a new respect for how this alpha took care of his pack.

I started to run. *But where to?* Other survivors emerged from inside parked cars and buildings. All of them covered with boils and wearing oil-stained clothes. Except it wasn't oil. It was blood. The streets echoed with the growls of Puppy and Alpha as they defended their territory. I should have left—they were just dogs—but would their cries alert Army Brat with her AK-47?

The Doberman crouched to the ground on his front paws when the creatures got too near. The dog butted his head into them, or leaped claws first, but he never attempted to bite. I took that as a warning not to let the survivors' blood or pus get on me, either. Greg's apprentice, Josh, stepped onto the street. We'd had him out to the house for repairs since, as my stepfather told us, he knew how to keep his mouth shut. He wasn't in as bad a shape as Greg, but his stomach looked as if someone had chewed it away.

How are you walking around without a stomach?

He headed toward the puppy. The tiny terrier looked from me to the left and then to the right. It circled, and darted between the survivors who were getting closer.

"Shit." I sheathed my machetes and took out my

slingshot. I had only a pocketful of marbles. Josh reached out for the terrier as I pulled back the elastic. *I could shoot the puppy, end its suffering here and now, stop the wailing for good.* The marble flew, cracking Josh in the neck. He looked at me but didn't cry out in pain or bring his hand to the wound or do anything that a normal person would do when shot in the neck. I wondered if maybe I had missed. But yellow pus was draining from where I had struck him.

Greg was still fighting the alpha when Josh wandered away from the terrier and started at me. I readied another marble, but a crash from behind reminded me that more survivors were coming. One glance over my shoulder told me I was in trouble. A mob had flooded the street around me.

The bodies surrounding my home were as decayed as the ones lumbering toward me. Their one thing in common: one bullet to the head. I aimed again, and this time I got Josh in the forehead. He went down. "Thanks, stepfather," I muttered. One shot to the brain was the only thing that killed them for good. I put away the slingshot. Not enough distance to reload. I drew my machetes. A few of those bastards were coming with me if this was going to be my death.

The damn dog was still wailing. Greg now limped his way toward me, so I ran in his direction away from the mob. I slashed out and lopped off Greg's head, and stood over the puppy. *If a shot to the head kills them, let's see how well they get on without a head!* This would be my last stand. I would die for something.

At first the survivors—no, not survivors, but creatures—circled me, as if trying to cut off my escape. As if they were working in a pack. As though they weren't completely mindless. But I had to think of them as mindless. I had to look at them as creatures; otherwise, I couldn't defend myself against them.

One creature rushed in to bite me, but I struck it with the machete down the side of the head. Not a direct head hit, but enough to drop it for good. Another rushed me from the side, and I dropped down to hit it in the kneecaps. The pain didn't even slow it down. I wasn't even sure it felt any pain. Surely not even these creatures could stand on broken legs! It toppled over with only one good leg left. As it collapsed, I hacked down on its neck with the machete.

Two down . . . but more were piling in around me.

If they rushed me, I'd be a goner in a matter of seconds. But they didn't. They each almost seemed to be waiting to see what the other ones did first. I couldn't help but compare them to the dog pack. I spun around when I heard a scream from behind me, and I saw a big creature lunging over me. But the Doberman had come back and tackled it. Teeth bearing down on the creature's neck, blood pouring onto the dirt road. I guessed we'd find out if the infection affected dogs. The creature struggled—*how are you not dead?*—but the dog wouldn't let go and the creature couldn't bite back. That skirmish diverted the other creatures' attention away from me.

One of them fell suddenly when a crossbow bolt slammed into its head. A second bolt followed. After that several more bolts dropped enough of them to make a path to one of the buildings—the credit union—ahead of me. It had a flat roof and, I hoped, access to that roof from the inside. There had to be people on the roof; they had just saved my life.

Children of Ruin

I grabbed the puppy before taking off, but it bit down hard between my thumb and finger. I stifled a scream. Noise would make me visible again. I forced myself to run toward the credit union's doors, ignoring the few creatures that followed. After pushing through the doors, I slammed them shut behind me. The only way to keep them shut as creatures pushed on them was to slide my baton through the door handles.

I was safe, for the moment.

CHAPTER SIX

The blood I was losing was the least of my worries. I had to see what was in this credit union with me. A few decapitated bodies were scattered on the floor. Above me, sunlight poured through a skylight much too high to climb to get out. No ladders. No ropes. Maybe there was a back door? The creatures were piling against the front door and had probably surrounded the building by now.

I clenched my hand, the sheering pain a reminder I was hurt. If I couldn't close my fingers, I couldn't fight with that hand. I wavered on my feet because the blood loss made me woozy. I was in trouble. The puppy backed away from me, growling. What was I thinking, grabbing the stupid dog anyway?

"Believe me, Pooch, I wish I'd left you to die," I said, without really meaning it.

What I needed was a first aid kit. Or for those creatures to stop banging on the doors. I wished I hadn't come. I wished I'd stayed in my hole.

That's because you're weak! my stepfather's voice said in my head. *If you want to have a place, you earn it!*

"I survived!" I screamed back at the voice. The puppy

stopped growling and cowered onto its back with its tail between its legs. "I SURVIVED!"

I swore I heard an echoing *plip* sound as the blood dripped from my hand and pooled on the floor. Without quick action, if this wound got infected, I'd be a goner. The creatures weren't the only danger in this new world. I needed a bandage.

I took off my leather jacket and the bike armor. I ripped off my T-shirt and tore a strip from it by standing on it and pulling as hard as I could. I couldn't cut it with the machete because infected blood covered the blade. I tied the strip around my wound and, using my free hand and my teeth, I pulled it as tight as it would go. I donned the armor and my jacket as quickly as possible.

Now what? Now you die? I heard my stepfather ask.

"No," I told the voice. I scanned the roof and tried to see how I might get up there. If others were up there, how had they climbed?

I moved about the credit union trying to get a better look. Trying not to notice the people crushing each other against the glass door. Suddenly a kid slightly older than I with a shaved head and dirty face appeared at the skylight, and we stared at one another.

He waved his arms and mouthed the word "MOVE."

This time when I scooped up the dog, he didn't bite. When I pushed myself against a wall, the glass came smashing down on the floor with a crash. Shards everywhere. I moved my back to the explosion, covering the puppy with my chest.

A rope lowered. I heard a boy's voice. "Climb up!"

Blood made my hand so slippery that climbing the rope was out. I grabbed it anyway and wrapped it around my good hand. Two kids stood at the skylight, the shaved-headed one waving me to start up the rope.

"I can't climb up with the dog!"

"Leave the dog!" the boy with the shaved head yelled.

"And my hand is injured! You need to pull me up!"

A worried look passed between them, as well as words I couldn't hear.

"Did you get bit?" a skinny guy asked, his voice shaking. He put a knife to the rope.

"By the dog, not by the people."

They argued again, so I yelled up, "If you don't pull me up, I'm as good as dead!"

The skinny guy kept his knife to the rope. A loud, high-pitched crack warned that the glass doors were beginning to give way.

The dog licked my cheek, and I wondered at my stupidity. Yet I didn't let go of him. He licked my face and wagged his tail a little as if finally understanding my sacrifice. The boys yanked on the rope and my arm wrenched as though it might snap from its socket. My feet lifted off the ground just as the creatures piled into the credit union. I rose just high enough so they couldn't reach me. The rope burned into my palm with every pull, but I refused to let go.

When I finally reached the top, I saw what looked like a linebacker pulling up the rope. The guy with the shaved head ran to help me onto the roof. My first instinct was to collapse onto my back, but I remembered they had almost left me down there. I held the dog in one hand and pulled out a machete with the other. My hand hurt from the rope, but I grasped the weapon with what might I had left.

"Cool, man. Cool," the bigger guy said to me. Now

that I'd gotten a better look at him, I saw it was Tom. Quarterback Tom. His lips parted into a smile as if remembering when he had beaten me up.

The guy who was going to cut the rope lay on his back, massaging his shoulder. He glared back and forth between the shaved-headed guy and me. Shaved Head held his hands out to me as if saying "Relax."

"If he's been bit and dies, we're all dead," Skinny said.

"I'm not gonna die," I said, knowing that I should have repeated, *I wasn't bitten.*

"You will if you don't let me tend that wound," Shaved Head said, nodding toward my hand.

"If we wanted you dead, we would have left you down there," Tom said matter-of-factly. I decided to call him by a nickname, Big Guy, just to push him.

I put the puppy down, and he backed up between my staggered feet. The cloth around my hand was bright red. I looked down at the credit union where several creatures were kneeling on the floor licking my blood. I slid my machete back into its sheath.

"Thanks," I muttered.

"When night comes, the deaders will wander off." Big Guy walked over to Skinny, offering a hand to hoist him up. Then he said with his back to me, "You can wander off then, too."

"You can wander off any time you want," the shaved-headed guy spat at Tom as he rifled through one of their bags. I caught a glare between him and Big Guy that told me they weren't friends.

"Scored from the credit union, lucky you." Shaved Head retrieved a first aid kit. He walked up to me, keeping his feet slightly apart, the knee on his back leg slightly bent.

Skinny sat against the retaining wall, rubbing the wrist of his hand that held the knife. I was betting Shaved Head had taken him down, and now he was ready in case he needed to take me down.

Shaved Head took out rubber gloves and put them on. "No glove, no love," he mumbled, and by his chuckle, I assumed it was a sort of joke. His lips trembled and his hands shook. That I was completely calm probably unnerved him. He unraveled my dressing and patted the bite with alcohol. It stung, and I cringed.

"So, you do have emotions. That's a good sign," he said.

"You're not doing this to help me," I said to him. "You want to see what kind of wound I took. Dog or human."

Shaved Head stopped, and his eyes grew wide. I wanted him to know he wasn't fooling me, just in case they had any other deception planned. They could tell me they had nothing to gain by saving me, but even that was a lie. They could learn the location of my shelter and scavenge my stuff.

"Dog, definitely," he said, examining the bite. "Have you had a tetanus shot?"

"Their blood got on me. Might have got on my wound." I wondered how smart I was to tell him that, but right then I needed to know this wasn't going to infect me. And if it were, I needed to know what to do.

"The virus only transmits from an infected's bite. How can you not know that?"

"And only human to human, else you'd be checking the dog, too," I mumbled to myself. Good news for when I ran out of food and needed to hunt.

Big Guy stared at the street, and Skinny sat against the

retaining wall. The pup was still beside me. Guess I was now its mom.

"You can't just blaze into town anymore," Shaved Head said to me. "You need to be smarter if you want to live."

When the world as we know it ends, you will be the first to die. My stepfather's words still cut, and now Shaved Head's words cut as deeply. I crawled back into that familiar little boy, helpless and scared.

I forced myself back. Shaved Head smiled.

"I saw that. Not as impenetrable as you want us to think you are." He gently punched my shoulder with his gloved hand, and it felt strange. I didn't know what to do when he did this. Say something? Punch back?

"You finished?" I asked and pushed him away. That felt most natural. He nodded, and I looked at the street below. "That's the infection . . . it drives people insane?"

"No." Shaved Head paused as if waiting for me to speak. When I said nothing, he added, "The infection just makes people sick until they die. What's down there is the people *after* they die."

I let that sink in for a moment. After? I remembered my stepfather talking about there being no after, saying that once we died, we were dead. Period. *This is why we must take what is ours now.* No after, no God, no right, no wrong. Just survival of the fittest in a world that existed for only as long as we drew breaths. *It is why everything I do is just,* he'd say.

"I don't understand," was all I could think to say.

"The Big Bang—surely you've heard of that?" Skinny Guy's voice dripped with malice.

"That started the world?"

"No." Shaved Head spoke first, interrupting both Skinny and Tom as they mumbled something I didn't quite get. "New Year's Eve last year in every major city in the world. When the fireworks started, someone in the crowd infected with the virus killed themself. The deaths happened hours apart, but they all woke near the same time. They started biting people, spreading the infection, so we called it 'The Big Bang.'"

People bitten by infecteds. They'd go to work, school, on play dates, whatever, even if they were unwell. No doubt some checked into clinics or hospitals—dying and rising and biting. Human ignorance of sickness used against us. Made sense.

"Who did this?" I asked. My stepfather would have believed the government—no matter what the evidence might have proven.

Shaved Head shrugged as he continued to clean my wound. "Some say terrorists, others blame the military. The world fell too fast and people got too sick too fast to really know."

"Where did all these people come from?" I asked, partly as a diversion but also actually needing to know this. "They aren't all townies."

"Were you in a cave when everything went down?" Big Guy said, as if I were just stupid.

Funny thing, I kind of had been in a cave.

"Some are doctors that were flown in," Shaved Head said. "Some are families that returned after moving away. Many people believed the rural, smaller cities would be safer. All it took was one infected to bring down the whole town."

"And the military," I said, wondering what would

52

happen when I met a deader wearing body armor.

"If I could update my status right now," Skinny said to no one in particular, "it would be 'Six weeks and the whole world is gone.'"

"You don't know that!" Big Guy sounded angry, as though they'd had this conversation before. For a short time, no one spoke again. I started to understand the horror I had been spared while living in my hole.

The edges of the mountains glowed bright orange as the sun disappeared behind them. As if beckoned, the creatures below started wandering off. Skinny paced back and forth. Big Guy sharpened a machete, the sound of metal on stone echoing against the darkening sky. A part of me wanted to take it from him and pound him into the cement—payback for what he had done to me when the world had rules.

Shaved Head continued to stare at me just as he had since they'd hoisted me up. "What's his name?" He nodded at the puppy at my feet.

I shrugged. I wondered if their encampment was close to mine. Were they low on supplies? Would they try to take mine? Was my stepfather with them?

"We could have left you down there," Big Guy said, as if giving a warning.

"Should have left you all down there," Skinny mumbled. "None of us would be up here if that army kid hadn't shown up."

I glanced over my shoulder as Shaved Head held up his finger to shush them. It made me think of when my mom did that to stop me from speaking my mind to my stepfather. My guess was Shaved Head was a college student, first-year education. He had that teacher vibe down pat.

"I had a dog before this mess happened," he said. "A Maltese named Spike. From *Buffy the Vampire Slayer*."

Shaved Head was trying to connect with me to build trust. *He needs to be scared of you. That will keep you safe.* I ignored my stepfather's advice and looked down at the shivering puppy. He was pressed against my leg, alert to every noise around him that we couldn't hear. He needed food. He needed water. Another mouth taking away resources. If I became friends with these other kids, they'd also become extra mouths to feed.

"Connor," I said with a throaty breath. The only thing I remembered about my real dad was his name, Connor. I don't know why I made that choice to call the dog after my real dad.

Shaved Head reached into a pack and took out an old, ratty towel. He walked close to me and kneeled beside the puppy. Connor growled as Shaved Head reached out for him. Shaved Head stopped, turned his hand knuckle-side up and let him sniff. Connor still growled, but when Shaved Head started to stroke his back, he calmed. He continued petting Connor as he wrapped him in the towel.

"He needs you to tell him it's okay," he said to me. I wondered if that was more about *his* needing to hear that from someone. I nodded, and he said, "I'm Oliver."

"Ethan." Speaking my name felt odd, like spitting out a weird meal I didn't expect to taste a certain way.

"We need to eat," Skinny said, "but I don't have enough food for everyone."

"I don't need your food," Oliver said back.

Children of Ruin

I thought about the machetes strapped to my back, the knife in my boot, and the slingshot in my pack. Oliver had had some training, so even though he wasn't the biggest, if I had to, I'd take him out first. Next I'd shoot Big Guy. And finally I'd take out Skinny. No doubt by that point he'd be cowering in a corner begging for his life. *It's not murder; it's survival.* If I wanted their food, there would be little they could do to stop me. Murder to survive was how my stepfather had trained me for this new world.

My pack was still on my back, so I slung it off to the ground. As I opened it, Big Guy took an interest. His hand clenched on his machete, and he waved his eyebrows at Skinny, who grabbed a metal bar. I rummaged around in my pack until I found the feel of two cold plastic bags. My MREs. I pulled one out and tossed it to Big Guy.

"I have enough food for all of us"—I gave the pup a pat on the head—"including Connor."

I was giving away too much, but they had saved my life. And a part of me didn't want war with these boys—not even Big Guy.

Big Guy dumped the MRE's contents and grabbed the biggest pouch, the beef stew. He tossed the crackers and peanut butter to Oliver, and the candy bar and gum to Skinny. It reminded me of my dad, keeping the lion's share because he considered himself most worthy.

Oliver looked at the crackers and made a *pshaw* sound, and Big Guy said, "What? I'm the biggest and need the most food!"

Oliver offered the crackers to me, but I shook my head and pulled a second bag from my pack. I took out the beef stew, and Connor stared up with eyes that told me he understood somehow this was food. I opened it, squeezed some onto the ground for him to lap up, and then tossed the remains to Oliver.

"Thanks," he said through lips that stuck from the peanut butter. The way he devoured the food, I was sure he hadn't eaten in a while. I sloshed the water in my bottle. I estimated it to be about half full. I poured some into my hand and let Connor lick it off.

"Maybe we could save the water for the humans." Skinny's voice was filled with that same condescension my stepsiblings had when showing me their new toys. *They are my favorites*, my stepfather had explained to me about his sons. *They are mine.*

I decided enough was enough. This wasn't my pack. I couldn't look out for people who didn't want my help. In this world, I had to stop playing by the rules I'd only wished existed in the last.

First, I considered my options. Big Guy was busy with his stew, and Oliver was watching me while smacking his fingers clean with his lips. Skinny scowled at me with that same mistrustful glare that I often gave my stepfather's sons. I approached him, holding the water out. His face scrunched for a second, and I jiggled the bottle to show him he could take it. He reached out, and when his wrist was close, I grabbed it and twisted his arm behind his back. He struggled, but I bent his wrist back and kicked out his legs so he was kneeling in front of me. My bottle fell to the ground, the water no doubt pouring out. I didn't care. Big Guy was up, but Oliver shook his head at him to stay put. Clearly they'd had a scrap, and Oliver had won. I leaned in close to Skinny's ear, making sure Big Guy could hear me as well. I growled, "What is mine is mine. If I choose to share, you just be thankful for what I give you.

You tried to leave me for dead, so I owe you nothing."

I kicked him in the back, sending him face first to the cement floor. He cursed but made no move to retaliate. As he stood up, he fished a puffer from his pants pocket and took three puffs. He wheezed but breathed steadily. Connor barked. Oliver picked Skinny up and patted his shoulders as if to calm him. Putting Skinny to the ground didn't make me feel better. Not at all.

"Do that again, and I kick your ass. For what, the third time?" Big Guy warned from behind me.

I ignored him and wandered to the retaining wall. I stared down at the walking corpses as they bounced off each other and filled what should be silent air with tormented moans. The deaders. A word that sounded saner than the unspoken one most appropriate: *zombie*. Could a virus animate the dead, imitate organ functions, and create a world of horrific resurrection? I thought about the comics and books I'd read. According to Zechariah 14:12, *"This is the plague with which the Lord will strike all the nations that fought against Jerusalem: Their flesh will rot while they are still standing on their feet, their eyes will rot in their sockets, and their tongues will rot in their mouths. On that day people will be stricken by the Lord with great panic. They will seize each other by the hand and attack one another."* Was I now looking at a walking risen army come to punish those left behind?

Connor's barking started the deaders over the wall returning to us. When everything was quieter, they seemed to reset to their original positions. I wondered why. Did deaders return to the place where they died? With dusk approaching, the sun's amber glow made everything look like a sepia photograph.

"I guess we're hunkering down here for the night," Big Guy mumbled as he watched the deaders.

"Right. I'm going to sleep here, trusting that you three won't either shank me or rob me of my stuff," Oliver said directly to him.

I caught a moment on Big Guy's face when it looked as if that comment had actually hurt him. Skinny just scoffed.

"Because you could possibly have anything I want," Big Guy muttered.

"Where are you holed up?" Oliver asked me.

Info I shouldn't share. They could have had others on the way for a rescue. But I knew they didn't, otherwise they wouldn't have come to the town alone seeking supplies. Nor would they have scrambled up here when the army guy showed up.

Considering the way they ate, I assumed they didn't have many supplies. I bet the stores had been pillaged long before, which made coming into town dangerous and fruitless. If there was even gasoline left in the cars, it would be the only thing still of value.

"Maybe we should have taken our chances that the army kid would have helped us," Skinny said out loud, and both Big Guy and Oliver nodded.

"Are you all stupid?" I put the emphasis hard on *stupid* to get them glaring at me. To get them paying close attention. "Did she look like she was checking for survivors or looting supplies?"

Big Guy crunched up the empty stew bag and threw it over the roof. No one answered me, so they all knew my words were truth.

"I have nowhere to go," Oliver admitted in a quiet voice.

"We've run out of places to find stuff. And we don't know how to grow anything," Skinny said, ignoring a hard glare from Big Guy.

"That true?" Oliver asked Big, who just nodded.

I knew Big and Skinny too well from school to know they weren't lying about this. Oliver was the wild card, the one who showed up in town last minute before the apocalypse. Kind of like finding that last restaurant at the end of the universe just before the end times come. If he'd wanted me dead, he wouldn't have fought Skinny to make Big Guy pull me up to the roof.

"Some are born great, some achieve greatness, and others have greatness thrust upon them." My favorite quote from William Shakespeare's *Twelfth Night*. For the first time since I'd found myself on the roof, I understood this might be my moment for having greatness thrust upon me—whether I wanted it or not.

"I can save you," I told them as matter-of-factly as I could. We had to act before the sun disappeared completely and the darkness made it impossible to find our way back to my home. We wouldn't know if we were attacked until it was too late. Escape needed to happen now.

"You can save us?" Oliver asked, smiling as though this was the oddest thing he had heard yet. Odder even than the dead rising to life.

"Yeah. I have a fortified home. Plenty of food stocks. And I can train you to protect us and to grow us all food. The question is, can you all trust one another as the same colony?"

"No, the question is," Oliver said to me, "can we trust *you*?"

"I knew him from school," Big Guy said. "He's weird, but I think we can trust him."

"If you want to be in my pack"—as I said this, I wondered where my stepfather had gone, and whether he'd found a colony too big for me to defend against alone—"I am the Alpha."

Oliver nodded and gave the other two guys a fierce look. They nodded, too, but only after a snort of disapproval. I now had an army of three. Four once I got Kady.

By now the creatures had scrambled in front of the credit union door, all cramming together. Shadows on the skylight told me they were also milling about inside the credit union. I wandered around the roof, looking down at the street. Deaders seemed to work in packs, and I watched as one moved and others immediately followed. I could have waited until it was nearly clear again, but how would I have gotten off the roof?

Connor pushed his shoulder against my leg and nestled back to the ground. Unless I left him behind, my options were limited.

"No one is coming for us," Big Guy said out loud.

"One of us has to lead the deaders away," I said.

"Don't get bit," Oliver said to me, his voice cracking in a high pitch as if he were jesting. As if any of them could survive a minute down there.

"Lower me down first, and let me clear out the back. There are stragglers, but I should be able to thin them out." I started to gather my stuff and took one more look at the pup. "I'll put Connor in my pack."

"That was sarcasm," Oliver said.

"And how do we know you won't just take off?"

Children of Ruin

Skinny spoke, immediately taking another puff. They were all just scared kids, not much older than I.

"He needs us, too," Oliver said. "That's why we can trust him."

"Meet me at the junction where Cariboo Highway meets Loon Lake Road," I told them. "Walk off the highway, through the hills. Stay out of sight of the deaders who follow me down the highway."

CHAPTER SEVEN

I thinned out the creatures at the back of the credit union with the slingshot. I didn't have nearly enough marbles to wipe them all out, nor did I want to waste too much of what I had. Oliver offered to shoot them with his crossbow, but I thought we might need his bolts later. Once we were all fleeing, we wouldn't exactly have time to risk retrieving marbles or bolts from the creatures' heads.

The boys lowered Connor and me. When my feet were firmly planted on the ground, I drew my machetes. The puppy on my back was heavy, and I worried what might happen if I got knocked onto my back in a fight. *Get to the dirt bike*, I told myself.

Fighting and killing the creatures was never an option. There were too many, and eventually one would get the bite that connected. The only useful things were two spilled tin garbage cans. The bags were ripped open, and flies buzzed around the rotting remains. I'd never expected the apocalypse to smell as bad as it did.

I walked over to the tins, took the lids, and glanced up at the credit union roof. The three boys still watched, and I was betting they were half expecting me to just sneak away. I could have. Being killed by deaders was a risk, and helping these three boys survive made them competition for supplies. I should have just let the boys die. Had they known the plan that was forming in my mind of how I could use them to take down my stepfather, they may have preferred that I left them to die on that rooftop.

Connor managed to squeeze his head out from the sack and lick the back of my neck. Hard to believe he was the same dog that bit my hand only a few hours earlier. I sheathed the machetes, careful not to slice Connor in the process. I ran a get-away course through my mind. Around the building, to Cariboo Highway, and straight out of town to where I'd stashed the bike. Question was, how long would the creatures follow before they chose to reset? And could they run faster than me?

It didn't help that Connor squirmed inside the pack. I heard him whimpering, and now I had to move fast. If he started barking before I was in place, the creatures would be on top of me fast. I crept around the building to Cariboo Highway, feeling the eyes of the three boys on the roof. I was reminded of what had happened after I was beaten up in the town. Of the shopkeeper who'd rushed out to help, yanking Tom off me.

There'd been shouting, and I just sat on the ground. My nose bleeding. Helpless as this pup in my rucksack. I didn't want it getting back to my stepfather that I'd been beaten up, so I'd crept away as the shopkeeper shouted it out with the bigger boys. As I stood on Cariboo Highway in front of that shopkeeper's store, I decided I wasn't going to be so quiet.

I didn't need to glance up at the roof to know that Big Guy was watching me so hard that his gaze pierced into me. I couldn't help but feel that he and I would one day come to blows, and I would have to kill him. Why save him, then? I had no reason to help these boys, except that in every comic I'd read, the hero never went back on his word. I asked myself the question I would ask a thousand times more: *What would Batman do?*

I held a tin lid in each hand. The creatures bumped against the credit union door. Once they noticed me, I would be committed. Ready or not. I breathed steadily. Sweat beaded on my forehead. I gritted my teeth. Then I banged the lids together and yelled. Connor howled. The creatures all stopped what they were doing and turned to me. Fresh meat. They started to run.

"Run!" Oliver yelled. I'd frozen, but his voice clicked my brain back into survival mode. I turned to sprint. Connor started squirming again and knocked me off balance. I swayed a little and turned to see the creatures gaining fast. By the time my feet were moving and I was running, I felt as if it were too late. Connor barked as if begging me to run, run, *run!*

I knew how quickly the creatures were gaining by the loudness and shrillness in Connor's barks. When I got to the bike, I glanced behind. None of the creatures had stopped, as they were all almost on top of me. I got the bike up and started it, and just as I sped away, the first hand was on me. Then a second, and a third.

But I was away before any of them got teeth anywhere near me. Maybe now that they were in motion, they'd just keep going until they eventually found someone—or something—to eat. I rode toward our rendezvous point.

The bike sputtered and rolled to a stop at Loon Lake Road. The puppy stuffed into my backpack squirmed and let out a frightened yelp. I climbed off the bike just as the pup kicked hard. He was moving into different positions as if trying to get comfortable. To coddle him would be to kill us both. Either I was his pack leader or he would become creature food.

I dropped the bag on the ground and opened it. The pup leaped out, shaking himself and spinning around to face me. Then he raised his shackles, bared his teeth, and let out a low growl. I knew he wasn't really growling at me. He was just confused and scared. I picked up the bag, grabbed the bike by the handlebars, and pushed it to the side of the road for better cover.

"Follow me or not, your choice," I said to the dog.

I glanced over my shoulder. Connor sat with his head cocked to one side. He had this dumb look on his face as his tongue lolled out the side of his mouth. I gave my leg a hard pat, and the dog came running to my side.

My stepfather would have been so ashamed of me. I remembered lying on my side in the woods the first time my stepsiblings hunted me. They hadn't touched my face, but they had kicked my back and chest. Because my lungs hurt so much I felt as if I were breathing underwater. I cried and wailed, hoping for someone to come and rescue me. I had run so far and long that I no longer knew where I was. If I hadn't found my way back, would anyone have cared enough to get me? No. Not that night, and not this day. The difference? I was no longer that helpless kid hoping his tears would save him—I was now the one in charge.

I decided to wait until I had counted to a hundred for the boys to catch up. If they were too scared to leave the roof, they might still be stuck up there, and I was at least the rest of the day's walk from home. What would happen if I waited too long and it got dark? If I used a flashlight, would that just be a summons for the creatures? Or more army brats? How safe would we be at Kady's, if the men who had tried to kill her knew we were hiding there?

Connor heard them first, but this time he didn't bark. He sniffed the air, letting out a low growl. I knew by the fear I sensed in his wide eyes that he sniffed deaders. I leaned down to pat his head.

"Good boy. That fear will keep you alive. Us alive."

He gave a good few sniffs at a ditch on the steep side of the road just before the woods on our right. I propped the bike on its kickstand and drew my machete and baton. My safest bet was to climb a tree and pick them off one by one with the slingshot. But as Connor scampered between my feet, I knew I had to protect him. I never should have saved him.

The rustling of bushes grew louder until it echoed all around me. I stayed focused on where the dog sniffed. The trees and wind could distort sounds from the woods. Connor's senses were more trustworthy than mine. I looked where he looked.

The first wail pierced my ears, and my heart began to race. I recalled asking my mom, "Are there monsters in the dark?"

"Yes," my stepfather would answer for her.

I thought of this as the sun beat its hot rays—and as the first in what looked like a dozen deaders spotted me. They had followed me from the town, going through the woods, a more direct route. *By accident or conscious decision?* I wondered. Once again, I transformed into that little boy lost in the woods, trying to hide from his older stepsiblings.

I remembered our game of hide-and-seek. Except

when they found me, they had beaten me up. The first time, I didn't fight back. I took the blows and shed tears hoping for someone to rescue me.

This was not that day.

The dog let out a howl as the first deader lunged. He was faster than I'd expected, but I ducked beneath his grab and sliced one of his arms clean off. Hacking off a limb did nothing to stop him. Before the next one came, I quickly sliced upward and lopped off his head. As it fell, two more scrambled to get me.

Run! my instincts told me. But if I did, I would have to leave the pup behind. I staggered my legs, and danced in a diamond pattern over him. This martial arts technique allowed me to face all four directions, and to protect both myself and the dog. My blades were like fans around me, ready for the next deader to lunge.

One grabbed my arm. I sliced his elbow. Another deader bumped the first one, and I cut both. Another deader grabbed my hair from behind, and as I was knocked off balance, I kicked like a mule behind me. My foot connected with a decomposed chest. But instead of knocking him away, my foot caved into his ribs. I was caught like a fox in a snare. I managed to slice his head clean off, but my foot stayed stuck.

More came. The pup cowered beneath me. My foot wouldn't pull free. I was as good as dead. A big deader rushed me and tackled me to the ground, and just as he was about to bite me, a bolt slammed into his skull. Had it gone clean through, it would have pierced mine. He dropped dead on top of me. More bolts cleared the area of danger, and I was saved from deaders. But in this world that did not mean I was safe.

I slowly looked over my shoulder. Oliver was standing with Big Guy and Skinny.

"That's twice we saved you," Oliver said, though I could see by his face that he wanted to say more.

I yanked my foot from the deader's chest and tried to ignore the slime that covered my boot. Instead of saying thanks, I remarked, "I was starting to think you three weren't gonna show."

Skinny and Big Guy were both scavenging the dead. Oliver knew I owed him my life. He stared at me, but what was I supposed to say?

I picked the bike back up and started to leave. Connor stayed close on my heels. Skinny and Big Guy followed, carrying a handful of stuff. From the looks of it, they had found a few flashlights and rings of keys. What did they plan to do with keys? I took out my notebook and wrote all this down. Afterward, I started for my home, choosing not to tell them about Kady just yet. For her protection, I needed to know for sure I could trust these guys.

On the walk back, the only noise was my stepfather's voice in my head telling me what a fool I was. *Everyone is the enemy. Eventually, there will be a fight for leadership—probably first with Oliver, next with Big Guy.* I ignored that voice as it told me to let them die now, rather than have to kill them later. I knew, as we trudged down the road, that his voice wasn't completely honest. My stepfather would have an army, and he'd be confident he was coming after only me—his cowardly son. I glanced behind at my army of three. My chance to survive the real threat: my stepfather.

The road curved into our driveway, with woods on

either side. I stepped around the rotting soldiers along the perimeter. Connor smelled them and froze. He barked high-pierced yelps and refused to go on any farther. This I'd have to train out of him. Grabbing the pup by the scruff, I dragged him with me. He would learn not to fear if I showed no fear.

"What the . . .?" Big Guy whispered.

When I turned back, I saw all three guys were frozen where the bodies began. They stared at me.

"It's okay, they're really dead."

"That's so not the issue," Oliver said.

"Well, *I* didn't kill them," I said, wondering if *that* was what I was missing. I let go of Connor, and he sat with his body pressed against my leg. He panted loudly and drooled on my shoe.

"Then who killed them?" Oliver asked. His tone reminded me of my mother's when she'd ask one of us kids something she already had an answer to.

"My stepfather." I was betting that wasn't the answer they expected. I started back toward the house, meandering around the bodies, with Connor only a few steps behind me.

"You're that crazy family that was on the news," Oliver said. "The cult that was stockpiling weapons for the apocalypse."

"It's getting dark. We should get indoors. Tomorrow we'll start to clean up," I said.

Eventually they all followed, muttering a lot of stuff that I couldn't make out. A plot to kill me? Concern that I was crazy? Did I need to point out that the apocalypse had actually happened?

"What's in the shed? Guns? Food?"

Big Guy's words were like sponges forcing their way into my brain. As they expanded, the pressure on my ears caused a ringing. I grabbed my chest, held myself tight and breathed.

"Never go in there! You will never go in there!"

"Wow. You need to seriously chill out," Big Guy said, as he thoughtlessly pushed his way past me.

Connor growled, but still stayed behind me. Big Guy opened the house door and walked inside, as though never considering there might be danger. That brashness would work to my advantage. I had no loyalty to him. He was an expendable; they all were. They could be the bait if they were naive enough to head into bad situations first.

I stepped inside after them and headed for the roost where I'd feel safe. I could see the entire territory, and though it was covered with bodies, at least they were staying dead. Connor couldn't make it up the ladder and whined until I shot him a hard glare. He sat, panting heavily. Oliver took out his water bottle and gave Connor a drink.

I took a seat on the sleeping bag, and my muscles started to ache. Running on adrenaline had drained me, and now exhaustion was settling in. Inside the house, the others rustled through the rooms. I heard whispered gasps—probably at the blood in my parents' room. Bet they were wondering if I'd killed them.

The others climbed up to the roost and sat against the rails. I turned to face the woods on the outskirts of the field. No need to be afraid. They could have just let me die had they wanted me dead.

"Do you have water?" Big Guy asked, his voice grainy.

"We'll have to take it out of the hot water tank. That'll

be the only clean water—and will only last us a day or two. We'll need to build a large filter for all of us."

They looked at me as if I had just spoken a foreign language. I didn't have to ask if any of them knew how to build one.

"Isn't there a lake nearby?" Big Guy asked.

"Yeah, but you have to filter and boil the water." I turned to face them, and when none of them spoke I took that to mean they didn't get it. "Parasites. Beaver fever," I explained, adding impatiently, "What skills *do* you have?"

"I can use Facebook," Skinny said. "Facebook status update: 'Off the roof of the bank, onto the roof of possible crazy man.'"

The other two snickered, and I wondered if that was meant as a joke.

"Facebook status update," Oliver muttered, "'Will learn to sleep with one eye open.'"

Skinny and Big Guy looked at each other and shrugged. Then they turned to Oliver, who stretched by pressing his back over the rails. When he stood up straight again he rolled his eyes.

"I'm good with the crossbow. I might be able to hunt. I wasn't exactly prepared for the world to end." He managed a wry grin. "Bet this still didn't wipe out my student debt."

I nodded. "We should beef up security. These deaders seem to stay put until put in motion—unlikely they'll wander over here. A simple wire fence might stop that if they do."

"I can do that," Big Guy volunteered. "I worked with my uncle repairing his fence on the farm every summer."

"That's a skill," I told him flatly.

"I'm pretty good at researching things," Skinny said more seriously. "I saw a library of survival books downstairs. I could give making water filters a shot."

Good. Keep them busy. I didn't tell them I'd memorized all the books. A water filter was easy; we'd just need layers of sand and charcoal. Several layers. The best thing would be a big drum for the water, like our hot water tank. The sand would filter out large impurities, and the charcoal would filter out the smaller ones. The water would get cleaner and cleaner as it passed through each layer. But we'd still need to boil the water so we could drink it. That was key. I didn't tell them this because I wanted them to do it. I wanted them to contribute—that would build loyalty.

Right now we had to burn the bodies, just to make sure there was no chance of disease. That could keep Oliver and Big Guy occupied. Afterward, I could teach them to grow things. It was spring, so we'd plant beets, carrots, chard, lettuce, and tomatoes.

But without knowing how contagious the disease was, could we grow anything where the bodies were lying? I took out my notepad and scribbled this all down. It was important to remember.

"We need to burn the dead," Oliver said as if reading my mind.

"My stepfather's supplies are in the cellar." I pointed so they knew where to look. "We should spend the night in the shelter. It'll lock, and we can all sleep."

"Is there enough room?" Big Guy asked as he eyed the house.

We couldn't all live in the shelter, and if we were going to be a colony, then we needed to move into the house. Survival was no longer about just me. And my stepfather had fortified our home for the apocalypse. As one unit, we should be invincible in this fortress.

"The house is a lot to defend," I told them. It would also be a lot to maintain in the winter, and I wasn't sure this crew was serious enough to do it. "Tonight the shelter. Tomorrow we figure out watch rotations so we can live in the house."

The sun was setting. The breeze had turned cool. I'd been on that bank roof most of the day, but they'd probably been up there for the entire day. Skinny was shivering. If he had heat stroke, there wasn't a lot we could do about it. Simple things we took for granted in the old world were now life threatening.

But tomorrow was another day. A fresh day. The first with the start of my colony, my army, one that I would use to take down my stepfather. Wherever he was.

CHAPTER EIGHT

I woke the next day in my shelter to the sound of Connor peeing on the floor beside me. I rolled onto my side and stopped myself from grabbing him by the scruff. Unless I took him right outside, punishing him for urinating indoors wouldn't make any sense to the dog. But I couldn't take him right outside. I didn't know what the three strangers might have been conspiring about while I slept, nor did I know if anything was waiting for us to open the outside hatch doors.

I flipped my feet over the side of the bed and pushed Connor away from his urine. I could stop him from tracking it everywhere, and at least the concrete wouldn't stain. I grabbed a rag from one of the nooks and threw it over his mess—just as he started to poop. That, I could just toss into my trash can toilet, which smelled as if it hadn't been changed in more than just a few days.

No time for a sponge bath or my morning routine. I had to find out what my guests were doing before they got themselves—and me—killed. I put on a pair of sweatpants, my T-shirt, and the bicycle armor. I grabbed my machetes and headed for the door, with Connor close on my heels.

Children of Ruin

I opened the door and saw the three cots, the sleeping bags on them unzipped with no one inside. A cool breeze whispered through the open cellar doors, and sunlight flooded the room. I stepped closer, cautiously. Connor tried to get ahead of me. I grabbed him by the scruff and pulled him back. He had to remember that I was the alpha male, else I couldn't protect him. The same for my guests, if they were still around.

As I placed one foot on the steps, I wondered if they had taken off in the night to get others. Maybe they had lied to me. Maybe they did have a colony set up somewhere. I could always move myself to Kady's, but what message would I be sending if I just gave up this place?

I finally reached the top step and looked outside. I heard them now, talking to one another. Mostly about how much better the air was without the stench. Did they understand they had left me vulnerable by propping open this door? Anything could have gotten inside.

Oliver was lying in the grass, propped up on his elbows. Skinny and Big Guy were throwing around my stepfather's sons' football. None of them had noticed me as I exited the bunker. I slammed the door shut, and the clang startled them all.

"What the hell?" Big Guy yelled as the football spiraled into his face.

"This isn't a game!" I yelled back. Connor made a show of it with a growl. I guessed his enemy was whoever I made out as my enemy. "If I can surprise you, anything could have gotten in there. And gotten me!"

"You were locked away," Skinny argued.

I started to regret bringing them back with me. If I

needed to undo this, I would have to kill them.

"We just wanted to air the place out—" Skinny said.

"It smells like ass in there—" Tom said.

"But you're right," Oliver said. The others glared at him, and I started to see this as "them" versus "him." He glared back at them and added, "We should have been more careful. We *will* be more careful."

Oliver walked up to me and placed his hands on my shoulders. It was awkward, and I wasn't sure how this action was supposed to make me feel. He looked directly into my eyes with his head tilted a little.

I glanced down at Connor. He was also looking up at me with his head tilted. The dog was curious, but that couldn't have been Oliver's intent. When he spoke, he did so with such a soft tone that I couldn't help but feel calmed.

"We're sorry we let you down. We're new to this, but you seem to know what you're doing. Please help by teaching us."

He smelled—and bad. He had dirt under his cracked fingernails and what looked like grease staining his face. Could have been deader blood. They all had it on their faces.

"I'm your only hope," I said. "You'd best remember that."

He took his hands off my shoulders and stepped away. I wondered if he was startled by my words or by the truth of what I had said. This wasn't high school. Being good at a sport, or dating a jock, or being the geekiest of the geeks was not going to make anyone king. All I needed to do was to get Oliver to trust me. Once he did, all of them would regard me as leader. A good start would be bringing Kady there, and getting her to tell them how I had saved her.

"I need to leave you all here for a day. The windows in the house are bulletproof, and the siding is fire retardant but not fire proof. There's a lookout at the top, but don't think you aren't vulnerable. The house is only safe so long as someone is keeping watch. Slack off even for a second, and it could all be over."

They all nodded, but only Oliver spoke. "Where exactly are you going?"

"To get someone I promised to help." I picked up Connor and handed him to Oliver. "Look after him while I'm gone."

"And what if you don't make it back?" The fear in Skinny's shaking voice was unmistakable.

"Then assume I'm dead. Do not come to rescue me."

Not that I believed my dying a possibility, but this was a good test for my three new companions. If I left them and they did well, that would mean I could leave them alone for longer trips and seek out other colonies. See who our competition for resources was, and possibly where my stepfather had gone. Once we established a real settlement, one with a garden and a few animals, maybe we could find trading partners. The end of the world could be the best beginning for the four of us.

I walked east down Loon Lake Road, thankful that it took less than a half hour to get to Kady's place. When I arrived, her hatch door was wide open. Of course it was. She was sitting on the grass with her hands clasped in her lap. When she saw me, she jumped up and ran toward me. I stopped when she wrapped her arms around my neck.

She was crying, and for a second I just stood rigidly. I remembered seeing my mom pat my sister's back once when she cried, so I tried that. It seemed to calm her.

"I thought you were dead," she said, sobbing.

"Clearly I'm alive." Even without anyone around to see her crying, Kady's affection made me immensely uncomfortable. "I found other survivors. We need to move you."

She pushed me back and crinkled her nose. With her forearm she wiped at her tears. "You obviously don't have showers where you live."

A murder of crows suddenly flew from the nearby woods. Kady jumped back. I stared hard at the tree line. Birds didn't fly out like that without someone—or something—disturbing them. *Could be something alive. Or something dead. Could be lots of people. Could be one.*

No matter what, we had nowhere to defend ourselves from if attacked. Too big a coincidence to assume someone might have arrived just when I did. If it were people, they would be waiting for me. They might even have run back to their colony to say I'd returned. My first instinct was to run.

Of course it is. You're a coward!

"I am not a coward!" I growled at my stepfather's voice.

Kady stared blankly at me for a second, obviously unfazed by the birds. She blinked before she said, "I never called you a coward."

I didn't even realize I'd spoken out loud.

"There's someone watching us. I don't want them to know we know. You need to pack a bag, and we need to leave."

Children of Ruin

"I don't want to leave. This is my home! All my stuff is here!"

"*Tom.* Tom is back at my shelter." This was the one thing I hoped would get her to listen. Head cheerleader, head football star. Just like Flash and MJ in *Spiderman*. It just made sense.

"He's alive? Does he know I'm alive?"

I shook my head and she slapped me. I wondered how we had gone from a hug to a strike.

"How could you not tell him?"

I would never tell her why, knowing Tom the way I did. A Tom she didn't know. Or rather, a Tom she chose not to know. The one who picked on kids smaller and weaker. The one who made himself stronger on the backs of those he considered beneath him. In a world like this, how could I know for sure that he wouldn't see all of us as weaker?

Kady didn't wait for me to answer and, as I'd hoped, she climbed back into her hatch. Whoever was watching might have realized we were onto them. We were paying too much attention to our surroundings. If it were a deader, wouldn't it have run at us by now?

With Kady, I'd now have four people to look after. I should have been worrying only about myself. *You'll be the end of us all*, my stepfather's voice reminded me.

But this time I didn't believe him. These others were key to my survival.

The walk back was more like what I'd expected an apocalypse to be like. Quiet, no people. As we walked onto the driveway that led to my home, I wondered what my companions were up to. A horrid feeling that I was about to find Connor dead and the homestead stripped bare consumed me. I stopped just out of gunshot range.

"I want you to wait here," I told Kady.

"But what if one of those things comes out of the woods at me?"

She was not wrong. These weren't like the ones in movies who wandered slowly. Some ran like track stars, and my guess was they didn't get tired in the same way we did. If their bodies could move even with half their chests blown out, then they must not have abided by the same laws of physics as we did. If one spied Kady, she was done for without me. Giving her a weapon was useless. Even if she knew how to use one, I didn't think she had the guts.

But since this was a small community, I doubted hordes of deaders were waiting for us anywhere. With some proper training, I could probably take this crew back to the town and clear out the few dozen we'd encountered the day before. The few left wandering the woods and farms and popping out of nowhere would always be of concern.

"You see anything, you just start running as fast as you can."

She nodded, and I started for the house. I considered drawing my machete, just in case. But I also didn't want to look like the crazy person returned to kill the colony. If I'd had my binoculars, I could have seen if anyone was in the roost. Now I would just have to find out the hard way by walking home.

I started over the field, keeping watch over my surroundings—the house situated atop a slight hill, surrounded by a field, surrounded by woods. One road in, which meant one road out. Anything else had to come by foot. I was within two hundred yards of the house when Oliver walked out the front door. Connor came tearing out the front door when he saw me and ripped through the grass until he was at my side.

"What the hell are you doing?" I yelled at Oliver, who stumbled backward a few steps at my outburst.

"It's okay. Blake is in the roost with a rifle. Shit. Relax," Oliver said, sounding exasperated.

"I've been watching you since you pulled up," Skinny . . . Blake . . . whatever his name was yelled down at me.

I waved Kady to come, and then knelt to pat Connor. He licked my face and jumped all over me—and while his happiness to see me made me feel good, this recklessness was going to get him dead. I grabbed him and made him sit.

"Stay!" I told him firmly, and he did. "Sorry. Just a little on edge, I guess," I said to Oliver just as Kady ran up to us.

"Oh my god, what's with the dead bodies?" she whispered to me.

"You could introduce us," Oliver said. He gave me a small smile, and then faced Kady. "Or I can do it myself. I'm Oliver." His voice was weird, as though he was angry. I didn't get why he was smiling if my bringing Kady there upset him.

"Kady."

I started for the house with Connor walking obediently by my side.

"We've been busy while you were away," Oliver said as he ran up to me. "We can make this place work."

I didn't cut off his enthusiasm by reminding him that

because this place was such a fantastic shelter it would become a major target. I followed him inside.

They had made themselves at home. Skinny and Big Guy had taken Kyle and Zeke's bunk beds; my cot looked untouched. I gathered Oliver had taken the master bedroom since they'd dragged the bloody mattress into the hallway.

"Oh my god . . . Kady!" Big Guy exclaimed when he saw her.

"Tom!" She ran to him and they hugged. Oliver started humming a tune as if this were some romantic movie. Big Guy shot him a dirty look.

"I thought I would never see you again," I heard Kady say as she and Big Guy parted.

Big Guy looked at me. "Why didn't you tell me you knew where she was?"

"Could you go meet Blake in the roost? I'll get Kady settled here," Oliver said, stepping between Big Guy and me, and leading Kady by the arm to my sister's room.

Big Guy kept his gaze steeled on me, and as I walked past him I said, "I was thinking of her safety, not about you." I climbed up the ladder to the roof, where Skinny was watching the area with binoculars.

"You're right, a fence would solve a lot of our safety issues," Skinny said when he saw me.

"We'd need supplies. It means a trip back to town—"

"No"—Skinny cut me off—"it means a trip to the city. The town was picked over weeks ago when all this shit started going down. Most people hit the electronics store first, but someone was smart enough to hit the hardware store."

My stepfather, I said to myself before Skinny finished

talking.

"They cleaned it right out."

"The city is too far. We can scavenge from our neighbors. We'll find the ones who didn't survive."

"We also need a generator," he said, "and considering how windy it is up here, we could run it off a wind turbine."

"And who's going to build that?"

"I think I can figure that out with all the books your dad left behind."

"*Stepfather.*" I said this firmly so he wouldn't forget. "Do we have all the tools you'll need?"

"I'm going to make a shopping list of supplies."

"That sounds reasonable. Then we'll go scavenging while the others stay here to keep this place defended."

I made a mental note that I was starting to lose command here. While their thinking for themselves was great, their making plans without asking for my agreement was dangerous. I couldn't tell if scavenging was a request, suggestion, or a command from them. It was still them versus me, no matter how congenial they might have seemed now.

"Make your list," I said in a very authoritative voice. "Then you and I are going on a trip."

He nodded, but after puffing on his puffer he said, "Maybe you should take Tom."

He was scared. He was putting up a good tough act, but when push came to shove he just didn't have what it took to survive. I watched him hold the rifle, and I was betting that, if he had to shoot it, he wouldn't know how to aim. Thing was, I couldn't leave him here. I had to take him because, of the three, I trusted him the least not to stir up trouble.

"You know what you need. You're the one who's coming. We can't make mistakes here. We'll leave tomorrow morning."

I didn't wait for him to answer. I grabbed the rifle from him and nodded my chin to the exit. "I'll take the next shift."

Keeping them busy had to be a priority. As long as they were working, they wouldn't be thinking about how scared they should be. And they should be scared.

CHAPTER NINE

Over the next few days, Big Guy and Oliver chopped down trees to make fence posts. I put barbed wire on the wish list, watching them from the roost with the relentless sun beating on us. Sweat beaded on my face as my pen scratched the dash code for *tarp* in my notebook. The summer was promising to be hot.

A patter of footsteps sounded up the stairs, followed by Skinny's voice. "I put together a water filtration system, thanks to those books your stepfather kept. No idea if it works. I used an old plastic garbage bin and cut holes in the bottom. I found charcoal and sand bags at the back of the shed and I made about three layers, each a couple inches thick. We can boil the water on the wood stove."

"You and I will trek down to the lake and bring back a few buckets."

He paused and his face scrunched up. I turned away to face the field so my command could sink in.

"How far is the lake?" Skinny asked.

"We'll want to get water where there's no chance of human contamination, so a ten-minute walk."

Even not facing him, I knew he was struggling with

this. Was he waiting to see if I was joking? Or did he expect the water to come to us?

"Do we have a wagon? A wheelbarrow? Anything to cart the water back in?"

I sighed. Not quietly, either. How had he survived so long being so lazy?

"No cart. No wheelbarrow. We have to walk through the woods. Be thankful there's a path."

"Every day? We'll be constantly going to get water!" Skinny yelled this at me.

Oliver's head perked in our direction. Of course, he left what he was doing to come see what was going on—as if he were in charge.

"And what do you suggest we do?" I asked calmly as Oliver joined us on the roof.

In my head, my stepfather whispered, *You need to kill them.*

"What's going on?" Oliver asked, stepping between us.

I imagined myself face kicking Skinny and knocking Oliver down the stairs. A simple rifle shot could finish Big Guy, and Kady would just cower back to where she came from.

"Ethan expects us to spend all our time running back and forth to the lake for water."

Oliver looked at me, maybe to give me a chance to explain myself. At this point, I was angry enough that I considered taking my stepfather's advice. Well, the advice my stepfather would have given me. About killing them . . .

Oliver turned back to Skinny and said, "The lake is where the water is. Where do you suggest we get water?"

Skinny started wringing his hands and stared at his feet.

"Go help Tom cut wood for the fence," Oliver said.

Skinny took the order and left me alone with Oliver. A part of me was angry that Skinny hadn't obeyed me so readily, but mostly I was impressed with Oliver's confidence.

"You need to build trust with them," Oliver said softly. As before, he placed a hand on my shoulder and gently squeezed. It calmed me.

"You all need to build my trust, too," I said.

He stepped around me to the rail and looked over the horizon.

"Kady is downstairs on the couch, sleeping. She needs to start helping," he said.

"You're going to suggest that she get the water instead of Skinny?"

Oliver's shoulders tensed and I knew I'd spoken with just enough disdain to piss him off.

"The two of them alone in the woods wouldn't last a mile. We need to consider our strengths." Oliver was right. It had never occurred to me that someone other than me would be putting consideration into how best to run our colony. For a second, I missed his hand on my shoulder. Only for a second.

"Big Guy—"

"Tom."

". . . is our only fighter. Kady and Skinny—"

"Blake. Do you really not know their names, or are you just being an ass?"

". . . could be taught to shoot. But if it came down to it, could they kill a person and not just a creature?"

"Could *you?*" Oliver's voice betrayed fear, and I wondered if he feared me or what this world might be making us into.

"Dammit!" Big Guy shouted from the middle of the yard, the sticks he was carrying dropping to the ground with a clatter. "I stepped in dog shit! Just because the world has come to an end doesn't mean you stop picking up after your dog!"

"He isn't wrong," Oliver said.

"He is. The world hasn't come to an end. We have."

Just as Oliver facepalmed, Kady screamed from downstairs. Her voice was muffled, as if she were speaking underwater. I started to suspect why she was about to be executed when I'd found her. There was a moment of silence, and then Kady's voice sounded again—but it was cut short by Skinny yelling back at her.

"You could have warned us about her before saving us from the rooftop," Oliver said with a smirk.

"She wasn't like that where she was living. She just needs to adjust." I didn't face him. Instead, I watched the field around the house, in particular, the roadway into the clearing.

"I'll take over for you on watch. Why don't you go downstairs and see if you can calm Kady down. Blake and Tom can take the night watches. Can we trust Kady to pay attention up here?"

Biting my lower lip, I placed a foot on the ladder. "I don't know."

I didn't trust any of them to pay attention in the roost, but I wouldn't last without sleep. None of them knew how to plant or harvest a garden, or hunt and trap food, or to defend themselves in a real fight. We needed to take time to train—before we ran out of packaged food or someone attacked us.

Children of Ruin

As I climbed down the ladder, the arguing got louder. The trouble with this strife was that it took our focus from survival. I had to send a message to everyone that I was serious about being leader, and that they had to listen to me. *Confrontation is a cancer, and cancer must be cut out severely*, I could almost hear my stepfather tell me.

Kady was on the couch, her arms crossed. Her face was tight in a pout. She reminded me of my sister whenever she'd want to play outside or get a new toy. Skinny was in the adjoining breakfast nook, and Big Guy was sorting through the stuff we had in the kitchen. The two guys were telling her she could be helping. Kady was yelling that she wanted to just go back home.

I walked directly to her, and she looked up at me through teary brown eyes. She opened her mouth to speak. I lifted her from the couch by the arm. She yelped and fought against me. I was stronger, and I forced her to the door and threw her outside. Big Guy and Skinny ran up behind me.

"This is how things are going to be from now on," I said, staring directly at Kady. "We are a team, one unit. Anyone who doesn't like it is free to go."

I brought her into the field, where I could see Oliver watching me from above. Connor was staying between me and the house, glaring at the other boys. He was definitely *my* dog. A part of me was mad at Oliver for not paying more attention to his surroundings, but he'd needed to hear that, too.

I faced Kady. "You want to go back to your hatch? You go right ahead."

I started back to the house, leaving her shivering outside. Connor followed me. Skinny and Big Guy were wide eyed and staring at each other. I glared at them, and then I spoke again to Kady. "When you're ready to join us, you're always welcome."

Even before I was able to take another step, Kady scrambled past me and into the house. When I was close to the guys, I said, "I'm going to cut wood for the fire. If you have any more trouble with her, remind her that staying here is a choice."

I turned and headed toward our woodpile to chop more wood. Safe. Alone.

Except that I wasn't alone. Connor was by my side, standing guard as I took a log from the pile and grabbed the ax that rested against the shed. I didn't need to see Connor's ears perk to know we'd been followed.

I took my log and walked to the chopping block. Oliver was now watching me.

"That was a real jerk move," he said in a dark, gravelly voice.

Kady appeared on the roof, watching us. She opened her hand and waved at me. I had no idea why, but I waved back if only so she'd stop.

"What you said to her was mean, even if it was needed. She won't carry the gun up there, but she offered to take her turn."

"Kindness is our enemy." I repeated my stepfather's words so easily I got chills. "We need to make her stronger."

Oliver sighed loudly. I ignored him and raised the ax. I brought it down hard on the log. The wood split in two. "Who's next on watch?" I asked as I reached for another log.

Oliver sighed, and I noticed his face soften. "Is that all

that matters to you? Watch for invaders, make a fence, scavenge food and water?"

I split the next log and another after that before answering. "Of course not."

"Thank god!" Oliver laughed and grabbed a log to sit on.

"We have to grow our own food. Learn how to make things again. Figure out a way to stay healthy. Sooner or later we're going to run out of things to scavenge."

"Didn't you have any hobbies before everyone got sick?"

"I collected *Batman* comics. I had nearly every one, including a rare *Detective* comic number twenty-seven."

Oliver nodded and watched me split logs. That he sat made me wonder if my show with Kady had any impact at all.

"Well, don't you still like to read those comics?"

"I only have thirty-seven comics left. The rest were destroyed." I realized by his long sigh that that wasn't what he had meant. "But yes, I would if I had more."

"And we need to still do our hobbies. Even if they are not important to you, our hobbies will keep us sane. They make life worth living."

"Oh." I stopped chopping wood and let that sink in before continuing. If it meant they'd work harder, then maybe letting them rest wasn't such a bad idea. He was right. I did enjoy reading comics, and I would like to count which ones I had left. Maybe I could scavenge the rest.

"What if we worked that into our routine, so there was always someone on watch while everyone else did their hobby?"

Oliver smiled. "I knew you weren't a Borg. I think we

can agree to that."

I ignored his Borg comment, mostly because I had no idea what that was. The scent of cooked oats wafting from the house distracted me, and I realized it must have been past noon. I stood beneath the rising sun, my arms suddenly sore and my mind on fire from all that had just happened. My fingers were starting to shake, and I slammed the ax down into the chopping block.

Oliver had already walked away from me and was circling the shed. I heard him fiddle with the heavy iron lock.

"Can we talk about what's in here?"

Images of what had just happened with Kady, the glares from Big Guy and Skinny Guy, and Oliver's soft, nearly condescending voice filled my mind until I felt as if I were going to burst. Then the jingle of the iron lock pierced my ears, like the sound of a hot knife cutting into my brain. I ran to Oliver, grabbed his shoulders and slammed him against the wall.

"I said never go in there!" I growled at him, slamming my first against the wood by his head. "Never! Never!"

"Whoa! Dude!" He pushed me off him but kept his hands up, showing me his palms in surrender. I fell to the grass, my own palms covering my ears so that the pressure in my head wouldn't split my brain in two.

Connor wandered over to me, slowly, sniffing the air as he walked. He pushed his forehead into mine and the pressure in my brain eased. He sat with me, his head pressed on mine. I glanced up. Oliver was watching, his eyes wide, his lips curled back.

"I hope to god you are not our only hope," Oliver muttered as he returned to the house. "Hope. To. God."

Children of Ruin

Over the next few weeks, Oliver took watch whenever Big Guy and Skinny Guy tossed the football back and forth. When Big Guy or Skinny was on watch, Oliver and Kady plucked blackberries from the vines near the house. Tom and Kady often went on walks. Eventually, our field was filled with echoes of laughter. A part of me wanted silence, to hide and to never be found, but wherever my stepfather was, he knew full well where we were. The laughter, if he heard it, would be daggers of victory proving he had failed to beat me. That he had not broken me.

We still hadn't scavenged, but I followed Oliver's advice and allowed my colony to get into a routine of work and hobbies. I found it hard to do, but something about Oliver made me want to ignore my stepfather's training. I practiced my Escrima with two bamboo sticks and taught Connor commands such as "stay," "come," and "hide."

He enjoyed too much of the chase game that Oliver sometimes played with him. I wondered if he would ever wind up in a situation where his instinct to fight was overcome by his desire to play. But on those occasions when a deader stumbled upon us, Connor froze with fear in a fit of snarls and growls that sounded like yelps. He smelled them long before they were a danger.

Today, Oliver was up on the roost, while Big and Skinny tossed a football back and forth. Kady was playing with Connor, running as he leaped at her feet. We each had one hour of fun—our "break time"—before we got back to work on important things. I was sitting in the grass, lost in my comics, until Oliver sat beside me. I looked up at the roost and saw Kady had taken over.

"What are you reading?" Oliver said to me.

I shrugged as an answer. Lately, reading my comics just made me remember all the ones I had lost. Hardly a hobby when it did nothing to relax me.

"You know what I miss?" Oliver asked as Connor ran to our side.

Oliver threw a stick, but before the dog chased after it he looked at me. I chose not to answer Oliver's question. I nodded at the stick so Connor would tear after it.

"Swimming. I miss being able to just go to our pool in the back and dive into the cool water."

Connor brought the stick back and dropped it at my feet. I didn't miss a lot of things about the old world—my stepfather, Kyle, and Zeke. And the hunts.

But I missed my mom. I missed my sister. I longed for the nights when my mom would come to my room when I felt as though my emotions were drowning me. She'd wrap me in a blanket so tight it would hold in everything that seemed to be spilling out of me. Those were things I missed. The creak of the swing as my sister wiled away her days imagining she could fly. So stupid it seemed then—but now I missed it.

"You gonna throw the stick? Connor looks like he might burst," Oliver exclaimed.

I threw the stick. Oliver watched me watching Connor. After a while I said, "I can help you swim." He sort of smiled at me, but with a weird, crooked-eyebrows-raised look that I didn't quite get.

"Forget it," I said.

"*I* want to swim! Where?"

I considered everything first. Kady was up in the roost,

without a rifle, but at least she was keeping watch. Big and Skinny were playing football, but they'd run to help Kady if a deader wandered onto the field.

I nodded at Oliver and headed toward the back of the house past the shed. He followed, as Connor closed on my heels. I took him to a spot in the back of the property that was a little overgrown with shrubs. Once we pushed past, we came to a path. Connor took point, sniffing that the way was safe. We walked until we emerged into a sandy clearing, at the side of the lake downstream from where we got our water. The water wasn't fast moving, and where we were, it was shallow and good for swimming.

To the right of us was a decrepit dock with a rowboat tied to it. It floated but had been there since before my stepfather bought the place. Who knew how safe it was.

Oliver rushed past me and jumped in the water. He didn't even take off his clothes. As I watched, his laughter reminded me of those rare times my sister laughed as I pushed her on her swing. I might not have ever taught her to fly, but this was pretty close for Oliver.

Days like this day would become our routine. Even when our supplies got dangerously low, and even long after we could no longer put off those things we had to do. But listening to Oliver's laughter, I knew he was right. Without these moments, what was the point of survival?

CHAPTER TEN

Because I had no natural light in my shelter, I had to check the clock for the time. Six in the morning, the twilight hours. I strapped on my machetes, and when I opened the door Connor walked to the top of the stairs, sniffed, and then tore outside. I followed him out into the field, stretching my back and staring into the rising sunlight. Steam rose from the dewy grass, and I knew it was probably going to be another hot day. I wondered what would happen to us when winter arrived. Would we be ready?

I lunged forward, stretching my hamstrings. My legs were sore, and I felt grungy. Oliver wandered outside with a steamy hot cup of something.

"Do you want a cup of hot water? We're out of tea," he said when he saw me staring at his cup. "We're low on water again, but we're always low on water."

"The built-in filtration system was dependent on our electrical systems running," I said, as I remembered the generator at Kady's. How could we bring it here? We'd need a truck. "Get everyone on the roof so we can have a meeting," I told Oliver. I glanced back at him, and he nodded.

Oliver went inside before me, and I remembered how

my stepfather ran meetings. He had always told me, *You don't need to respect me. You need to fear me. Fearing me will keep you alive.*

That had turned out to be a lie. I remembered reading *Lord of the Rings*, and what ultimately made everyone loyal to Aragon. He acted like their servant before he became their king. I just had to figure out how to do that. Not that I wanted to be their king.

Once everyone was up on the roof, I joined them. "We need to figure out a way to pump water to the house. It's time to scavenge."

Skinny Guy started fidgeting. I remembered my stepfather yelling at me for doing that, telling me people only did that when they were nervous or afraid. "Oliver and I are going scavenging," I said.

They all nodded, perhaps because they knew the chances of us coming back were slim. Skinny stopped fidgeting. No one wanted our job. Oliver said nothing, and I wondered if that thought was on his mind, too.

"How will we know if you two get killed?" Kady asked, her voice trembling.

"You'll know because we won't come back." Oliver said this quickly, and I remembered his shock when I had said something similar to him only a couple months before.

"Should we give a time limit before coming to look for you?" Big Guy's voice trailed off in the end, making me believe he didn't want to come after us.

"Carry on as if we're not coming back." Oliver said, his words echoing what I knew was true.

"Shut up!" Tom said.

"What's the problem, Tom?" Oliver spoke before I

could tell Tom to get bent.

"No, I mean be quiet. There's a girl crying."

We all listened. Sure enough, beneath the whistle of the wind was the soft sobbing from a small child. I couldn't help but remember the soft voice of my sister, especially on those nights when my stepfather tucked her in. A stab of anger and regret pushed that memory from completely surfacing.

I peeked over the rail and saw a little girl swaying back and forth on the rusty swing set. She was clinging to the chains, and her head was down so that her long, unkempt black hair covered her face and chest. The tips of her toes barely touched the ground. She kept herself swinging by gently kicking the ground once in a while.

"Where the hell did she come from?" Tom asked.

A smile flashed on my lips, and my eyes swelled when I recognized her. *My little sister!*

I wanted to run to her.

"I have to go to her," I said, against my better judgment. All that mattered to me was that she was my sister, and she was alive.

"We'll all go," Oliver said.

"No. Watch the roost. Someone must have brought her here. Watch Connor."

I started down the steps but couldn't help feeling like a little boy being led to something that I should be able to see. Every step was heavy as I approached the front door as if I were being transported back to before all this had happened.

When we were little, my sister would spend hours on the swing set. She loved it so much. And sometimes when my stepfather was out training Kyle and Zeke, I'd push her as if launching her all the way to the moon. It was the only time I ever heard her laugh.

Remembering her laughter made hearing her weeping seem weird. I took a step forward out the front door. When I was on the stoop, I stopped. Something was wrong. When I was a few yards from her, she turned and looked so fast I stumbled in shock. I fell backward. I tried to get my wind as I slammed back against the ground.

Her face. Patches of black skin. Bloody eyes. I scrambled to get up. She started running to me. Not a full-fledged run, but a half gallop—almost a skip. Her leg was broken. Her fingernails were muddy. Her clothes were soiled.

Panic hit me. She was getting closer.

A gun fired.

"No!" I screamed to my friends on the roost.

As the shot rang out, hollow screams erupted from the woods. As if people were screaming by breathing into their lungs and not exhaling. We were surrounded. My sister flew to the ground as the bullet hit her chest. I couldn't see anyone else around me. Just my sister. Lying motionless on the ground. Smoke rising gently from her chest where the bullet hit. My hands shook.

"You have to get back up here!" Oliver shouted.

But this was my sister. She was not some casualty that deserved her fate. She was the one piece of innocence I couldn't save. Thoughts of running into the shelter took over me, but echoes of memories froze me from action. First, all I remembered was running from my stepfather shooting at me from the roost and screaming to myself, *I must save them!* But the soldiers were on us, the ones I had led. My stepfather had turned to fire at them, and they'd fired back at him. If I had paused to find my sister, my stepfather might have had time to lock himself in the shelter.

The memory ended, and I whispered, "Sorry."

I took a step forward. Another step and another. Long grass covered my sister's body. I heard the worst of the screams. They began with a moan, echoing in the clearing against the wall of trees that surrounded my home.

"Ethan! You have to come back inside!" Oliver yelled at me again, his voice high-pitched.

When I was nearly by my sister's side, she started screaming. Slowly, she sat up and opened her mouth. As she rose, her voice got louder, until it pierced my eardrums. When she was fully standing, she stopped screaming. Her jaw locked in a snarl, her rotted teeth grinding as black saliva dripped from her lips. Her fall had twisted her broken foot. I couldn't imagine her pain. I couldn't imagine anything left of *her* in that body.

As she got closer, the stench of her rotted flesh made me gag. I remembered not to let her bite me. I drew my machete from its sheath, tucked my hand beside my left ear. She stumbled toward me, teeth gritted, eyes like two gray marbles. No emotion in her. As if she wasn't aware of what she was doing. Maybe she wanted me to kill her.

I swung the blade left to right in a downward arc, slicing her head clean off her shoulders. At that moment, I hated my stepfather for making me so good at this.

I fell to my knees as a hand rested on my shoulder. It was Oliver's, and he was shaking me.

"They're here! You have to RUN!"

I sat there, staring at my lifeless sister. I expected her features to soften, the color to flush back into her cheeks.

To see any sign of a person return. But even after I decapitated her, her face stayed like stone. Frozen in a twisted expression of anger. *Not a person. Not a person.*

When I looked away, I saw at least two dozen deaders walking in a mob, all heading for me. Somewhere in the back of my mind was Oliver, still screaming for me to get back into the house. But the fury rang so loudly in my ears that all I could hear were my footfalls pounding the ground toward the deaders.

Shots rang out, and a few deaders collapsed to the ground, their brains exploding out the back of their heads. When I reached them, the gunfire stopped. Neither Big Guy nor Oliver was a good enough shot not to hit me.

I sliced a deader in the knees, and as it fell I hacked deep into its scalp. The others fought each other desperately to be the first to get to me. I downed two before my adrenaline burned out. I realized what I was in for. Too many. Too close. My colony could not help. Once again, I was that helpless boy in the woods my stepsiblings were hunting. I was alone.

Bolts chunked into their heads, and the deaders started to fall. Oliver was a dozen paces behind me. He cleared off enough so that I could run back toward the house. As I did I heard Tom in the roost, finishing the rest off with the rifle. I walked back to my sister, where she was still lying dead, and I collapsed to my knees. Emotions pushed their way up into my chest. I fought them down. I couldn't feel. I couldn't allow myself to feel.

"It wasn't her," Oliver told me, as he rested his hands on my shoulders.

I didn't move. The pain growing in my chest kept me locked kneeling on the ground. Oliver slid his hands around my shoulders and, kneeling, he hugged me from behind. His head rested in the crook of my shoulder. His tears were on my neck. He squeezed me tighter and tighter, as if he were trying to squeeze out the pain from my chest as he would water from a sponge.

And the pain did flow out, as a wetness down my cheeks that dripped onto the brown grass where my sister would be set to rest. I vowed this would be the last time I would cry.

My stepfather had kept shovels, hoes, and gardening rakes at the back of the house, all leaning against the wall. After several minutes, I grabbed a shovel, walked a few paces from the swing, and started digging. I shoved the tip of my shovel into the hard, cracked dirt. Dust rose into the air, some flying away on the wind and some covering my shoes. Oliver and Tom muttered behind, discussing if they should help me.

I would dig the hole six feet deep and four feet long. My sister would finally rest in peace, probably with my mother. That she'd rest beside her swing comforted me somewhat. Me being the one to put her there was fitting, since it was where she and I had played together and stolen moments of joy. Conner trotted over to me, sat with his head tilted, and watched. Oliver brought a shovel and started digging.

"No!" I grabbed his shovel and shoved him. "I didn't ask for your help!"

I didn't wait for him to react, or speak, or say anything. I expected him to wander off, maybe complain about me to his buddies. At that point, with my shovel sinking into dirt, with the reeking scent of my sister's decayed corpse beside me, I couldn't have cared less.

But he just stood there. Watching me. Leaning on his shovel. I dug up a few more clumps, and Oliver started again. I blocked his shovel with mine, and then hooked the edge of my scoop in his and pulled it from his fingers. Then I kicked it away.

Oliver looked over his shoulder at the shed, and squinted at me. He walked to his shovel, picked it up, took a few paces back toward the house. He sighed so loudly that I was sure he meant to tell me how frustrated he was by me. I kept digging.

But then Oliver came back, and when his shovel hit the sod, I stopped.

"What do I have to do to make you leave?" I took a few steps toward the house, where Kady watched from the roost while Big Guy and Skinny dragged bodies into a pile. "WHAT DO I HAVE TO DO TO MAKE YOU ALL LEAVE?"

Big Guy and Skinny turned their attention to Oliver. When he just kept on digging, they kept on with what they were doing. I held my shovel so tightly that my knuckles turned white. I wanted to stomp the ground, to throw the shovel at Oliver, and then scream at the sky. But Oliver just kept digging. And Big Guy and Skinny kept piling the deaders. And Kady just kept watching the road. So I returned to the grave, and started digging as well. Softening the dirt with my tears.

CHAPTER ELEVEN

I checked my compass to make sure Oliver and I were headed in the right direction as we made our way through the woods. The trees were our best cover, not from the deaders but from the two surviving camps that we knew of—my stepfather's and the army brats'. The fellow hanging at the gas station was probably a warning for the brats, telling them that Clinton was now the One-Eyed King's territory. That they didn't listen told me they had firepower. Whatever firepower they had probably made them believe they had little to fear, but they didn't know my stepfather the way I knew him. They had much to fear.

Connor walked close to my side but sniffed the air and ground as we moved. His tail was up and wagging, so I knew he wasn't sniffing any deaders. The walk was steady and quiet, except for the sloshing of water as Oliver's bottle slapped against his leg. He had it hooked into his belt for easy access, instead of in his pack like mine. While he seemed calm when we were with the others, he kept glancing around the woods at every noise. For me, walking through the woods felt no different than my training sessions. Something scurried in the bushes nearby and

Children of Ruin

Connor dashed after it with a bark. Oliver readied his crossbow, spinning toward the commotion and sending his water bottle smashing into his leg.

"If you accidentally shoot Connor, you and I will have a problem."

"Sorry. A little nervous being out here after yesterday."

"If you're nervous because of me," I paused and caught the words in my throat, "I'm sorry."

"No, as much as you probably should, you don't scare me." Oliver smiled and gave Connor a pat on the head as he trotted back, having failed to catch his dinner. "When I saw you save this one, I knew you were one of the good guys."

On hearing that term, *good guys*, the memory of my stepbrothers' blood on my hands made me aware that no matter my penance, no matter the good I might do, nothing was ever going to make me one of the good guys. We said no more to each other as we continued to the end of the woods in back of the Jeffersons' very modern, white-wood-siding, two-story home. Large glass windows, big patio. Impractical for an apocalypse.

Before we left the safety of the woods, I checked my notes to remind myself what we were looking for: fence post driver, wire for a fence, gears, and something to use as a windmill. Canned goods and maybe some toiletries were unlikely bonuses. The Jeffersons' farm had a crop duster and was the best place to scavenge gasoline and tools.

I put out my arm to stop Oliver. As he bumped into it, I felt a vest of some sort. He was smart enough not to speak. We both just listened. I should have been hearing chickens, ducks, cows. Instead, I listened to the whisper of wind against the poplars behind us. I glanced at Connor, who was completely calm—so I knew no deaders were nearby.

"Someone has been here," Oliver said.

"Someone might still be here," I told him. No deaders didn't mean no one was here.

As we walked toward the house, I was more and more certain there would be nothing left to salvage. If the livestock were gone, chances were so was the gasoline. As we neared the house, my primary concern was that Mr. Jefferson could still be alive. If so, he might be desperate to defend what was left of his home. More so now than when the scavengers before us had come.

Oliver walked up the steps first. I didn't stop him. This could have been a trap, and better he was caught than me. The doorjamb was splintered, probably from a crowbar. Confirmed our suspicions that someone was here. No bullet holes—so no gunfight.

With the butt of his crossbow, Oliver pushed the door open, and it creaked on worn hinges. If anyone—or anything—were inside, they would know we were there. Oliver's nose wrinkled and he gagged a little. Connor whined, but he wasn't freaking out. As Oliver stepped inside, the stench of decay reached me. It reminded me of my shelter, and I felt a sense of safety inside the darkness. My eyes took a second to adjust. The Jeffersons, one of the wealthier families, had a state-of-the-art home. All the gadgets and luxuries of the Modern World. About as useful now as a lead boat.

As we moved into the living room, I sighed with relief. At the same sight, Oliver gasped. We had just found the whole Jefferson clan, each family member dead on the floor.

"There are times when I wonder if it's a blessing I survived," Oliver muttered.

Mrs. Jefferson and the two kids had bullet holes in the tops of their heads. Dried blood had soaked into the carpet—I couldn't tell where one pool stopped and the next began. If this had been a murder-suicide, Mr. Jefferson would have shot himself beneath the chin to guarantee a clean shot through his brain.

While he did appear to have a gunshot beneath his chin, he also had one in the top of his head. Just like the others. Someone had forced them to their knees and shot them through the top of the skull. I stepped over the blood and picked up Mr. Jefferson's arms, pulling down his sleeves to see his wrists. *Rope cuts on wrists. No suicide.*

"Shit, don't you have any respect?" Oliver gasped. He pushed me away from the bodies. Connor growled and jumped between us.

"They're dead. The killers are long gone, and we'll have nothing left to scavenge here."

Oliver's eyes were wide and glued to me as I started for the door.

"Killers? He obviously killed his family and then turned the gun on himself."

I paused at the door before going back out into the sun, astounded that Oliver couldn't see what I did.

"The blood splatter under Mr. Jefferson is wrong, and he has two bullet wounds. Whoever did this was sloppy, and didn't realize the second shot from beneath his head didn't exit the first. There are also cuts on his wrist from when they tied him up. Someone murdered this family, probably for their supplies, but didn't want to alert others who might happen on them."

"Why would they care? There aren't exactly cops to worry about."

"No. But they may want to do the same to us if they find us. This way, when they come, we still wouldn't be expecting them."

My hope was that Oliver would start to understand why I needed him and the others to stay on watch and to train. I took a sip of water from my nearly empty bottle. This gave me an idea.

"Their hot water tank might still be full, and the water in it will be clean. We should fill our bottles."

"How can you be so cold? This is horrible!"

"We need water and supplies. How is that cold?"

"People died here! Take a second to be shocked, or sad, or something!"

"Tears won't bring them back. Fear will get us killed."

Oliver tried to speak, but tears were forming in his eyes and the words stuck in his throat. Getting emotional about this was a waste of time. The Jeffersons were nothing to me. Did Oliver not understand that we might have had to do the same if they'd been alive when we arrived? Or if the Jeffersons had happened on us, wouldn't they have been as ruthless?

I wondered what we would have done. If the Jeffersons had fought us, how far would we have taken it? Would we have executed them? *You would have. You were once mine*, I heard my stepfather say. But I wasn't my stepfather. *I might have offered a peaceful trade alliance.*

From the living room, we could see a large glass patio door off the kitchen. It was closed and probably locked. Doubtful anyone else was in here, unless they were upstairs. I wondered if the Jeffersons had put up a fight for their resources, or if they had just refused to join another colony.

"You check the kitchen. I'll go upstairs and check for medicine."

I didn't wait for Oliver to follow; I just started toward the stairs. If there was a clean mattress upstairs, we needed it to replace the bloodied one in my parents' room. I wasn't sure how we'd get it back to our camp, unless we were lucky enough to find a truck with a tank of gas.

"Wait," Oliver put his hand on my shoulder, "I'll check upstairs. You check the kitchen."

What difference does it make? I thought to myself.

He wiped tears from his face, and I wondered if he hoped there'd be tissues upstairs. I didn't say anything and walked toward the kitchen. Connor followed close on my heels. The cupboards were bare, and the electricity had been off for so long that whatever was in the containers in the fridge had gone bad. Connor walked straight to that scent, but whined and sneezed at it before walking elsewhere to sniff.

Our footprints had streaked the linoleum flooring. Those were the only markings. Whoever else had been there had made sure to clean up their mess. This was targeted. The other possibility was that the previous intruders were still here. Had there been any mud when Oliver and I arrived? Couldn't recall. We hadn't been looking for it. Were men still in the house, and had they scrambled upstairs to avoid being seen? I didn't hear Oliver, and I wondered if I'd sent him to his death. *Better*

him than you, my stepfather would have said.

I took the stairs slowly, with my machete held close to me. Connor was in front of me, sniffing every step. If there were any men in there, they wouldn't be diseased— they'd be fighting back with weapons. Connor might not react the same way as he did with deaders, but hopefully he would react.

The top stair turned onto a landing, from where three more steps led to the top floor. I was in the center of a hallway—two closed doors on the left, and one closed door on the right. Sound, like a toilet flushing, was coming from the door down the right hall. I walked toward it.

Just as I was about to push the door, Oliver swung it open. He screamed and fell back into the shower. The curtain broke off the rod. He was caught in it.

"Shit! What is your problem? Were you listening out there?"

"I thought you might be in trouble, so I came up to help."

Oliver stared at me for a few seconds, perhaps to decide if I was telling the truth. He glanced back and forth between me and Connor. "I looked inside the other two rooms, but closed the doors again. The toilet works if you pour water into it." He gestured at two pails filled with what looked like dishwater as he took to the stairway. "They saved their brown water."

I realized he was upset that I had startled him. Actually he was probably embarrassed. But would he rather I had just let him die when I thought he might be in trouble?

"I'm sorry," I called after him.

He was already nearly out of the house. I didn't expect him to hear. He did. At the doorway, he stopped and turned to face me as I stood halfway down the stairs.

"I need you to communicate better. Tell me when you are going to do something, and maybe offer a teaser as to why. Maybe, just maybe, you could show a little pity, too. These people had families—they were your neighbors. You're acting like you don't care."

I shrugged. I considered putting my hand on his shoulder, but it didn't seem as if that would work this time. All I could think to say was, "These people never did anything to help me, or my dead mother, or my dead sister."

"Oh. I never saw it that way," Oliver said.

As I stepped past him, he wrapped his arms around my neck, and I swiveled, ready to kick his knees out. But he'd done this slowly, gently, and I wasn't sure it was an act of violence. He didn't react to my struggle. He pushed his head into my neck and placed one of his hands, again gently, on my back. He squeezed.

"Have you never had a hug before?" he asked.

"No," I told him. I mean, I was sure I had before my mom remarried, but I was so young, how could I remember? I didn't know what I was supposed to do, so I just stood there with my hands at my side. Did this make him feel better? Was it supposed to make me feel better?

"No one ever felt pity for you, did they?"

"Do you want me to hug you?"

Oliver laughed in a way that seemed to exhaust the tension between us. He let me go and punched my shoulder. "No."

I took out my journal to write this all down. The Jeffersons, the scavenged farm, the importance of a hug to ease tension. As I was writing, Oliver wandered into the yard toward the big red barn. Connor settled by my feet. I wasn't sure what the hell had just happened between Oliver and me—but I had a feeling it was significant.

I ran to catch up, nearly tripping over Connor. We carefully made our way to the barn to check for more supplies, hoping that whoever had been there first hadn't known what to look for. The barn wasn't locked, and the doors were wide open. No animals inside, though the smell of their presence still lingered.

We looked behind the barn. There was a plane. Intact, but too large for us to take back.

"You know how to fly one of these?" Oliver asked me.

"No, you?"

"No."

"Whoever was here before us got what they came for. Animals, food, and most likely medicine. If we check the farm's gasoline, I bet the drums are empty," I said.

"So, what now, General? Not a lot of anything useful here."

"The propellers on the plane. Possibly the alternator in the engine. What we need are batteries, gears—"

"For?"

"The wind turbine that Skinny will build us."

"Stop being petty. Don't call them stupid names." He gave me a look that told me I was crossing a line.

"Blake. Whatever."

I opened my notebook to my list of supplies Skinny needed. In the barn, I spied a rusted bike with gears we could scavenge. If we took our time, we could drag a couple of the propellers back with us. I looked Oliver up and down, and couldn't help but think he didn't have the muscle—or the energy—to pull something that heavy. He saw me sizing him up and blushed.

The sun started to fade as my mind worked this out. We needed a safe place for camp. A part of me wanted to stay in the house, but the stench of the dead was a little much, and those days one couldn't always count on the dead staying dead. There was the coop and the barn. The barn was too big to hold should we fall under attack, and the coop was just too small. Staying outdoors was also out of the question.

"Hey, General"—Oliver spoke in a tone that I was fairly sure was mocking—"you want to let me in on that private conversation going on in your head?"

"What are you talking about?"

"Your eyes are darting everywhere, and your forehead is scrunched the way mine gets during an exam. I'm wondering what's going on."

I nodded and found both comfort and concern knowing he wasn't as clueless about me as I'd hoped. It could be that he was trying to lighten the situation just so he didn't feel uncomfortable traveling with me.

"Let's sleep in the house. We can choose one of the rooms, and barricade the door. It's been hit recently, so we should be safe at least for tonight."

"Agreed," Oliver said, as we headed back to the house.

I woke before my watch, but it took a moment for my eyes to adjust to the candlelight. Connor was fast asleep on the floor at the foot of the bed, and I decided to let him sleep. Oliver was standing by the window, and I could see by his reflection that he was sobbing. My first instinct was to scold him for standing by an open window—he might as well have had a target painted on his chest—but I just couldn't. Whether I liked it or not he'd become Robin to my Batman, and like the Dark Knight, I had to take care of him.

"The world didn't change for you all that much, did it?" Oliver asked. He wasn't facing me. I assumed he saw I was awake from the reflection in the window.

"Life is pretty much the same for me," I said, confirming his suspicions.

He smiled a yellow-toothed grin as he turned to face me, and I made a mental note that we all needed to start brushing to stay healthy. Cavities could cause a bacterium that led to weakened hearts and disease.

"That may be the first time you didn't skirt a question."

I shrugged. He walked over to the bed where I was lying. My machetes were on one side of me. He lay on my other side. The mattress was small, and he had to edge right up to me to fit. I thought he believed we were bonding. He continued to stare, and even after I closed my eyes, I felt his gaze boring into me.

"Better that you watch our surroundings than me," I said, without opening my eyes.

I heard a scoff in his tone as he said, "Too dark to see anything anyway."

Even with the world ended, I was reminded of how different I was.

"Maybe you should tell me why you fear everything," I said back, trying to imitate the tone people had when joking.

His body turned rigid, and when he started speaking again, he seemed on the verge of crying.

"I came home halfway through my first year of

university after all my profs got the virus. After my parents died, it was just me and my sister. The grocery stores all closed down when the trucks stopped bringing shipments, and we were running out of food. Next, the electricity shut off and the telephones. We didn't expect help any time soon.

"When two men came dressed as telephone repairmen, I was so overjoyed that I let them inside. They had no tools. When I asked them about it, they claimed the tools were in the truck. First, they needed to check the jacks. When they saw my sister, and what food we had left, they told me they were taking it all. I threatened to tell the telephone company, and they just laughed. That's when I realized they weren't with the telephone company."

Oliver paused. He turned over on his side so his back was to me. I could hear him sobbing quietly, and then he said, "They stole our food, and . . . beat me and my sister. After that, after the men left, she died and I was all alone."

As Oliver wept, for the first time I understood that, as hard as my life was, it wasn't the only hard life. I remembered him hugging me, after we'd argued earlier, and how he'd thought that would make me feel better. I wondered if that might help now, so I reached an arm around him and squeezed gently. At first he was awkward, as I had been, but then he relaxed and intertwined his fingers with mine. He still wept. But eventually, in the safety of my arms, he relaxed.

"No one will ever harm you again, I promise." After I had whispered this, he moved his head so it rested on my shoulder. Having him so close gave me comfort. I felt . . . safe.

I remembered my stepfather yelling, "There is no safe!

In the darkness, you will be prey or predator." But the lesson he'd offered wasn't for me. It was for his sons, as I stood on the edge of the woods while the last traces of the sun disappeared. It was cold enough that I could see my breath. I was only wearing sweatpants and a light sweater. Kyle and Zeke were wearing full camo jackets, army pants, and steel-toed boots. Nothing was on my feet—as though I were an animal and not a person.

"You need to hear and smell," my stepfather continued to instruct. I shivered, but not from the cold. He was going to push me into the darkness, and I was scared of what I'd find. Or what would find *me*. I was like Bruce Wayne falling into his cave of bats.

My stepfather threw a bucket of water on me. When the water hit my eyes it burned and I smelled of vinegar. I rubbed my eyes, but that just worsened the pain. I tried to force my eyes open, only to feel a slap across my cheek.

I face-planted right to the ground. Tears flowed freely, and I started to whimper. I dared not let myself cry.

"You will hear him, and you will smell him." My stepfather spoke only to Kyle and Zeke, as if I were a creature that couldn't think. "You will hunt him, find him, and bring him to me."

I wondered if my stepfather would have been so willing to teach my stepsiblings with me around had he known how closely I was listening. How much I'd been learning.

The candles fizzed out, casting Oliver and I into darkness. Before I could move off the bed for my watch, Oliver grabbed my arm.

"No one will come," he whimpered.

I closed my eyes to sleep. He wasn't wrong—no one was going to find us here. Probably. He held me beside him, and I decided to just stay.

"One day," he said in the darkness, "you're going to have to tell me why you feel no fear."

I didn't know why, but when he said those words, I instantly had an image of the shed in my mind. Of my stepfather dragging me into it. Of my mother crying from the doorway of the house as she watched, helplessly as he closed the door with us inside.

CHAPTER TWELVE

After breakfast, Oliver and I took to the road east of Loon Lake toward Evergreen Resort, a series of cabins city people rented in summer and winter for fishing and the "wilderness experience." The resort also had a store, and with any luck it was far enough east that the army brats hadn't discovered it.

Oliver stayed more than a dozen paces behind me, and every time I turned to look at him, he diverted his eyes. I wondered if I should say something, or if that'd just make things more awkward. I tried not to think about it since we had a few more days on the road, thanks to the water we had found in the Jeffersons' hot water tank. Hopefully we'd find more at Evergreen Resort, even some from a pump that we could boil, and then we could continue farther.

We came across a farm a few miles from the resort. The field was green, which meant someone had been irrigating it. We heard the sounds of cows and chickens, none of them distressed. The soft cluck of chickens as we neared the farm meant survivors. It was now midday. Once we spied the coop, we spotted an elderly woman throwing seed down as a dozen chickens pecked the dirt around her feet. I grabbed Oliver and pulled him into the treed area that surrounded the farm.

"What now?" Oliver said, though his voice didn't peak at the end like a question. "Just sit and wait?"

I opened my notebook and looked back through the pages until I found an entry that fit.

Before the Fall, they were well known for their animals dying. They were from the city and never learned how to feed or care for them properly. Rarely did they have crops that didn't fail. They were proof that Google couldn't solve every problem.

"If they're peaceful, they could be a trading partner. An ally," Oliver said as I read.

"They're old. Someone will come along and kill them eventually."

Oliver shot me a harsh look, and I realized he thought I meant us. "Maybe they'll accept our help," I added quickly. My words were followed by a machine-gun blast.

Oliver and I hit the dirt. The woman who had been attending the chickens fell to the ground, and the birds clucked wildly around the spilled seed.

On the opposite side of the fence, a man dressed in camo, carrying an assault rifle, crept into sight. I scolded myself for not realizing we could have been trailing the army brats all along. They had been at the Jeffersons' and, as we were, they were making their way to the resort.

The army brat used hand signals to someone behind him. We waited, and three more dressed the same followed ten paces behind him. I remembered the one I'd found in the town. Somewhere nearby, there had to be a military base—possibly set up when the infection began. Maybe at the resort—

"What do we do?" Oliver whispered as we listened to gunfire inside the farmhouse. Several shots fired for maybe half a minute, and then nothing.

"We stay hidden. And hope they don't take everything."

We watched. Four went in, but only three came out. Two were carrying bulging hockey bags. Hope that there might still be something left for us dwindled. Maybe we'd get lucky and the bags would be filled with body parts and not anything valuable.

I crept from the trees, Oliver following close behind. I held out my palm as a signal for him to stay put. He did. Slowly, I crept to the chicken coop. All the livestock had been left behind. The woman was on the ground, a ring of blood around her head soaking into the dirt. The basket she'd been carrying in the crook of her arm was now crushed beneath her. Seed mixed with her blood.

I waved for Oliver to follow, and we hurried to the house. This wasn't going to be pretty, but hopefully Oliver wouldn't experience the same level of shock as the day before when we'd found the Jeffersons. As we neared the house, Oliver pulled me to a stop.

"One is still in there. What if there's more coming?"

I nodded. There could have been so much stuff they needed someone to stay as lookout. I drew my machetes and approached the front door. It was ajar, just enough that I could peek inside.

Even if I hadn't seen the blood, I would have smelled it.

I silently stepped inside onto a shag carpet soaked with something sticky. Bullet holes riddled the walls—one of them from a 12-gauge. And then I spotted the owner of the home, collapsed against a wall, still clutching his gun. The home had been ransacked, but quickly. I walked into the kitchen. Oliver took to the upstairs. The cupboards still had china and silverware. Useless. But I found some spices that I threw into my rucksack.

I heard a sound, like the one my sister made when she sobbed herself to sleep. That muffled voice of a little girl trying to stay silent. It was coming from a cupboard beneath the sink. Someone was inside. Oliver was still upstairs, and a part of me thought I should wait for him. But if this were the army brat, she could be armed or even radioing for help. I tapped the cupboard door with my machete.

"You may as well come out. If we wanted you dead, we would have just fired through the door."

A pause, and then the door creaked open. A little girl no older than five or six crawled out hands first. She was dirty with matted hair. Before I saw her face, I wondered if she was going to be a deader.

"P-p-pwease don't h-h-hurt me," she said, as tears cleaned a path down her muddy cheeks.

I sheathed my machete just as Oliver joined me in the kitchen. He pushed past me, and I noticed his full rucksack.

"Hey, you're okay now," Oliver said to her. "We're the good guys." To me he said, "The fourth soldier crawled up the stairs before bleeding out."

He walked slowly to her and kneeled beside her. He stroked her hair.

She slowly looked up at him.

"Oh god," I heard him mutter.

"Whatsa matter?" the girl asked, through a whimper. Oliver's face flashed innocence as it changed from concern to casual. He didn't have to tell me what he had spotted.

Slowly, he rolled up the girl's sleeve, and we both looked on a nasty bite that was oozing infection.

"What bit you, honey?" Oliver asked, his effort to mask his fear not well hidden.

The girl collapsed to the floor. She couldn't stop blubbering. She was definitely scared. Barely, we were able to make out words such as "brother," "bit me," and "dad shot." It was enough. We couldn't take her back with us—but we also couldn't spend a whole lot more time here.

"Stay here a moment, okay, honey? I just need to talk to my friend."

The little girl nodded, and Oliver and I headed into the next room.

"What now, General?"

I knew what we should do. She was dead anyway, so it wasn't murder.

"It would be," Oliver told me directly to my face. "I know how that mind of yours works, and you can spin it any way you want. We kill her, we're murdering her."

"We take her back with us, we may be killing everyone else. Murdering *us*."

"We can't just leave her here," Oliver said to me, leaving us in stalemate. The world was gone to hell, and the decisions we were making were tough. Truthfully, we could just leave her here. We didn't have to kill her. Those army guys were coming back, and by then she'd be so scared she'd try and trust them.

"We take her with us. We try and clean the wound, maybe quarantine her for a week." I heard the words coming from my lips, but couldn't believe them.

Oliver wrapped his arm around me and gave me a hug. He whispered thanks.

I didn't go with him into the kitchen. My mind was racing as to how I could go back on what I had just said.

But when Oliver returned with the girl's hand in his, I couldn't say no. Silently, we marched back toward our camp. A march that felt like a green mile.

Back at the colony, the first thing the girl did was point at my sister's swing set. Oliver told her she could play later, and I looked to the roost where I saw Big Guy watching with the rifle strapped to his shoulder. He saluted at me, most likely not to say hello but to show he'd seen me. I saluted back.

"Careful, you'll become friends," Oliver said, with a hint of mockery in his words.

I wondered if he was playing the Peter Parker of our group—quick-witted and holding a secret that made him long for revenge.

The girl wandered off to the swing. I started after her to stop her. Oliver rested his hand on my shoulder and shook his head no. "I'll look after her. You do what you need to do."

Before joining the girl at the swing set, Oliver ran inside the house, and returned wearing gloves. I recalled the first time he had tended my wound. He was gentle and knew what kind of bite it was. He was the right person to attempt to treat the little girl. The right person to decide if we could save her—or if the infection had coursed too far into her blood.

"What's going on?" Kady asked, as she rushed beside me. She kneeled down to scratch Connor behind the ears.

"We found this little kid hiding in a house. Stay away

from her. We think she's been bitten."

A pause in the conversation was all I needed to know that Kady agreed with me that bringing the kid here was stupid. But the tone of Kady's voice when she next spoke told me she agreed with our compassion.

"I'm—I'm going to go on a water run with Blake."

Kady ran off quickly. I couldn't blame her. I didn't want to be there, either. Not because I was scared of the little girl; I wasn't. But because I didn't want to be the one to make the ultimate decision if Oliver couldn't. My sister's grave was just to the left of me, and I had a flash of having to bury this other kid beside her. My guts turned into knots. I knew I just couldn't do it.

I could still check out Evergreen Fishing Resort and see if anyone were holed up there. Or, if the army brats had stripped it clean of anything useful. I could take the short way through the woods and along the lake, and be back before the end of the day.

"Connor, you and I need to get out of here for a while."

Connor barked as if in agreement.

CHAPTER THIRTEEN

Connor and I wandered into the woods toward a deer trail not far from the colony. It led to the other road that was less traveled—the one that ran alongside the lake and didn't pass any cottages or homesteads. I hadn't taken it with Oliver for the same reason I knew the army brats would never take it—we'd never find anything to scavenge.

The woods were quiet and cool. Connor was rushing to keep up with me, sniffing at the air. As long as he was calm, I knew I was safe from deaders. Where the trees were thinner, the sun burned down on me. *Sunscreen.* One more thing to add to the list of items we needed. I tried to stay where the leaf canopy protected me, as I had to find out who else might be there. In a situation like this, even friendly people could turn deadly when their resources disappeared.

I pushed through the woods, slapping at mosquitoes and brushing away spider webs. Connor stayed close behind me but was not as adept at moving silently through the brush. He would learn. As I hacked at the branches with my machete, clearing as much of a path as I could, I felt like that little boy, not so long ago hiding from his stepsiblings. A cornered lamb, forced to become the lion.

Where are my sons? My stepfather's voice echoed in my head, as it had a month earlier.

"I had no choice!" I screamed back, but not in my memory. My voice echoed in the woods, with only a murder of crows taking flight to answer me. Connor tilted his head. I got a grip on myself, pushing the memories down. *I am not that boy anymore,* I told myself over and over. I had not been that boy since that day . . .

Cows mooing interrupted my thoughts. The animals sounded calm, as if people were caring for them. Cows at the resort? Someone had brought them here. I needed to know if the army brats had, or someone else. Whoever it was, I couldn't assume they were peaceful. The law made most people kind—and now there was no law.

Metal creaked in the gentle breeze. When the creak was at its loudest, I came to a meadow where I discovered more than a dozen swaying gibbets—iron cages suspended from trees. A decomposed corpse, sometimes several, with flies buzzing and feasting, was inside each one. The flies so numerous they sounded like an airplane motor. I hid my face in my palm, hoping to filter out some of the stench. It didn't work, but I pretended it did.

I paced along the row of cages until I found one containing a man who was still alive. He was unconscious, breathing in heavy rasps. Connor rushed below and sniffed the cage. I watched to see if he'd yip and flee. He didn't. I looked up to another nearby cage and examined the body inside. Black from decay, with skin hanging from the bones. His jaw was open, and he had no teeth. I looked at the living man and wondered if it would be the same with him.

Children of Ruin

Using one of my machetes, I poked the live man just to see if he really was alive. I longed for the time when the dead stayed dead. I glanced down at Connor, who paced around the gibbets, sniffing. He wasn't whining, or fearful in any way, so maybe these men weren't infected. I used the blade to open the man's mouth. He made a sickly sucking noise, as if his jaw were stiff as a rock. Black ooze dripped from his lips. I saw only blackened gums. I couldn't help but feel as though I were walking into a trap.

Connor suddenly burst into barks and growls. Not at the man in the cage, but at the forest around us. I drew my other machete and waited. I was expecting deaders, but instead two army brats emerged from the trees. One was taller, with long blond hair and no weapons. The other, pointing an AK-47 at me, was shorter but very broad and well muscled.

"We checked them already," the blond kid said, "they're staying dead."

"Connor, heel," I said sharply, and Connor stayed at my side. His teeth were bared, but he was quiet.

"I'm Timothy. This is my associate, Gareth." Timothy held out his hand, but I stayed where I was. I scanned the surrounding woods for signs there might be more of them. "You dumb? It ain't polite not to at least say 'ello."

"Hello-who-are-you?" I said, all in one breath.

"I told you who I am. You daft? You belong to that colony at the resort, yeah?"

Gareth brought his hand onto his pistol. I saw signs of people hidden in the trees. Shadows. At least two I could see. And only one of me. Suddenly I wanted to write this down. I reached into my pocket for my notebook, and Gareth took his pistol out of the holster. I showed him it was just a notebook, and he and Timothy both relaxed.

"Oi! You don't have to write down where you're from," Timothy said with a snort.

"I'm not," I scribbled down the numbers so I wouldn't forget, "I'm not telling you where I'm from."

Timothy snapped his fingers. Three girls emerged from the woods, all carrying AK-47s. My chances had slipped from slim to none—and my mind raced fast to consider other options. If I attacked, they'd mow me down before I hacked off one limb. Connor could distract them, and I could get away. But then I'd lose Connor. I wondered what the chances were of some deader just wandering over to us.

Slowly, I bent at the knees and placed my knives on the ground. When I stood back up, Timothy nodded at Gareth, who took out a pair of manacles. When Gareth grabbed my wrist, I twisted his arm and kicked out his knees. I clicked the cuffs on him as he collapsed to his knees on the ground in front of me. Timothy's crew cocked their guns and aimed them at me. Or rather, at us.

"Let him go!" Timothy yelled at me.

I crouched behind Gareth and made myself a smaller target. Connor got behind me like he understood. I grabbed my machetes, sheathed one and pierced the other into Gareth's side so that he cringed.

"Tell them," I said.

"He has a knife and is sticking it in my side!"

Timothy burned red with anger and shouted. These kids were playing war and treating life as though it didn't matter, but they weren't running off a plan of any kind.

"I'm going to disappear into the woods. Gareth is coming with me. When I'm safely away, I'll uncuff him and set him free."

"No!" Timothy yelled at me. "*I'm* in charge!" He stomped his feet and threw a tantrum. A memory flashed through my mind of my sister not wanting to eat her vegetables. That time, my sister had brought out the wrath of my stepfather.

"Your other option is that I slit his throat, and you come pick up the pieces."

"Uncuff him now!" Timothy screamed at me.

Two shots fired. Two of Timothy's soldiers splattered blood from their forehead before going down.

"You're not alone." Timothy swung toward the woods with his gun.

In fact, I *was* alone. But he was right about someone else being in the woods. Someone who was neither an army brat nor one of mine. I knew exactly who had come.

I whispered to Garrett, "If you want to live, you have to do what I say."

Just then, my stepfather emerged from the woods with six of his colony behind him. They weren't carrying assault rifles, but they did have hunting rifles capable of taking us all out.

"Who the hell are you?" Timothy asked, glancing around the trees surrounding us. He was smart enough to know more people could be hiding.

"Who am I?" My stepfather spoke with an arrogance as if everyone should fear him. "In the land of the blind . . ."

"The One-Eyed Man is King!" the people with him all shouted in unison—including those still hidden in the woods.

"I bet you know who I am, yeah?" Timothy spat. "I own the stockpile of weapons the army left behind when everyone died. You don't want war with me, mate!"

The chuckle from my stepfather sent rivers of fear up my spine. Suddenly I couldn't help but become that little boy forced into the woods. Hunted by the sons his stepfather loved.

"Garrett, when I say run, if you want to live, you better follow me," I whispered to him. I knew I should use him as a shield and get away, but this kid was innocent and just following whoever he believed had the greatest chance to survive. Right now, that was me.

A gun fired and I felt Garrett slowly drop dead from my grip. My stepfather was pointing his pistol at me—I hadn't even noticed him take aim with it. Now I was completely exposed. Dead.

"Boy, it ain't our time yet," my stepfather said, without taking his one good eye off Timothy. I knew he still spoke to me. "But when it is, your death will not be quick. It will not be simple. It will be a masterpiece."

"What the blast is going on? You—don't move!" Timothy pointed his gun at me, but someone fired from the woods, right at his toes.

"I'm going to let both of you live," my stepfather said. "Make no mistake. I am letting you live only so you can see your compound given to me without a war. Given to me, because I am the rightful heir to this land."

"Why would I give you my compound?" Timothy asked.

I turned to leave and slapped my leg so Connor would follow. I didn't see what exchange happened, but I heard my stepfather's men all shout, "Because the One-Eyed Man is King!"

His blind followers. Them, he could lead into any fire

he wished. Even to Hell itself.

When Connor and I returned to our colony, everything was quiet. I stopped at the tree line and listened for Big and Skinny's football games, Kady's complaining, or Oliver's orders. But the field was eerily empty, covered with a heavy silence. I readied my blades in case of deaders. However, Connor sniffed along the ground calmly as he found a place to make his mark. As I approached the house, no one greeted me from the roost. For a sickening second I wondered if the army brats had beaten me back to the house. Maybe they knew about us all along, and now everyone but me was dead.

Imagining Oliver dead sent a rage into my blood so that I shook uncontrollably. The thoughts of scavenging on my own, of the constant worry that someone might take over my home when I had to sleep, of being all alone when my stepfather finally launched his attack—all this pushed a pain into my chest like a great weight. I imagined back to when I had discovered the bloody sheet in the master bedroom, and how wrapping myself tightly in it seemed to squeeze out this pain.

I took out my notebook and considered writing down what was wrong, but as I stared at the blank page I didn't know what to write. I flipped back a few pages to when I had met my crew, and rubbed my fingers over the names. *Oliver, Blake, Tom, Kady.* Should I cross them off, maybe tear out the page and pretend they never existed? Was it my fault if they were dead because I'd never forced them to train properly?

The front door to the house was closed. I stepped

carefully, one foot before the other on a sideways approach. I turned the door handle slowly so that when the door opened it made no noise against its hinges. Inside the home was as quiet as outside, and I knew no one was there—at least no one alive.

First, I checked Oliver's room. Empty. Then, Skinny and Big Guy's. And finally, Kady's. No one was home. I was alone.

"H-hello?" called Kady's voice from the front door.

I rushed to meet her. I saw her cheeks were smeared with grime and tears. Connor stopped beside me.

"What happened? Where's Oliver?" I asked, prepared for the worst.

"Th-the girl," Kady began through broken sobs, "you better get to the lake."

I burst through the doorway and dashed for the lake. I crashed through the path that led from the edge of our clearing through the woods to the beach. Big Guy and Skinny were kneeling beside Oliver, each with one hand on Oliver's shoulders. I stood silent. And listened to Oliver's gentle sobs. He sat in the grass, his gun cast aside. His head slouched and his shoulders jerked up and down. He was sobbing over the dead girl in front of him.

Kady rushed past me and kneeled beside Oliver, tucking her head against his shoulder. Oliver stroked the girl's hair, her blood pooling where the bullet had entered her forehead.

"I–just–wanted–her–to–see–the–water–before . . ."

Kady let Oliver go as his voice broke into sobs. Big and Skinny stood. As they all walked past me, they patted my shoulder. Oliver turned to me. His face tear stricken and his mouth open as if to speak. Though his lips moved, no words sounded. But I could make out him mouthing, "You were right. Oh god, you were right. I can't. I can't do this. I can't."

I kneeled beside him and wrapped my arms around him. I squeezed him tight, the way my mother's sheet had held me tight. To push the pain out of him.

"You should have let me do it," I whispered in his ear. "You should have let me be the one—"

He buried his head into my shoulder so hard that I had to stop speaking. Now he understood me a little more, and on those occasions when I'd have to act to save us, he wouldn't think it came easily to me. He would understand all the emotions I didn't know how to show.

While I held Oliver tightly, I looked at the girl on the ground nearby. The bandages lovingly wrapped around the bite mark on her arm made me wish that Oliver had been spared this truth for just a little while longer.

CHAPTER FOURTEEN

Oliver, with an emotionless smile, watched Big Guy shovel the last bit of dirt over the girl's grave. We didn't even know her name. All we had was a cross we'd made from two sticks to remind us that she had ever lived. My memories drifted back to the day before when Oliver had seen me wallowing by my sister's grave, and how he'd gotten me moving to make me feel better. He had refused to let me sink into despair. No doubt that had saved my sanity, as a result.

"Let's go for a walk," I said to Oliver. "Now is the perfect time for us to check out Evergreen Fishing Resort."

Kady was standing on his right, and Skinny was in the roost. Both were shooting me hard glares, which I ignored.

"Maybe he'd like a moment," Kady growled back at me.

"No," Oliver said, "I don't want a moment. Ethan's right. I need to do something."

Oliver took my hand, and I followed him to the house to get our packs. Big Guy gave us a weird smirk. Inside the house, I refilled our bottles, and Oliver emptied the previous day's haul from the packs and onto the living room floor.

"They can sort this out," he mumbled. "Where to?"

"We'll take the short way to the resort," I told him. He took my hand again, and when our skin touched I felt him shaking. "But there's something I need you to see first."

We left the house and I pulled him toward a path. We headed down it until we came to a high log, which we leaped over and began making our way through dense woods.

"Where are you taking me?"

Without answering his question, I took him through the woods to a cabin in a clearing. Most likely poachers had built it, thinking no one would stumble upon it this deep into the woods. The same reasoning my stepfather had used for choosing this location for his hunts: no one would ever catch him. He had never counted on a cabin being here. Had never counted on the leg traps I'd find inside. Or me having the conscience to do more than simply wait for my stepsiblings to find me. Me drawing them to the cabin. Drawing them one at a time. To prove to my stepfather that I was as good a hunter as them.

"What is this place?" Oliver asked as he slowly walked around it. He ran his fingers over the duct tape on the shattered window. He looked up at the moss growing on the roof, and tapped the log walls that were stacked tight. A good three-yards of dirt separated the trees and the cabin. Oliver wandered around the cabin and I stayed still by the trees. I waited while he walked to the back. Where he would discover what I wanted him to find. Connor sat on my feet, impressing me with what a good guard dog he was fast becoming.

"Oh. My. God," I heard Oliver say from the opposite

side of the cabin. "Weren't you taking me for a walk to get my mind off this shit?"

I wandered slowly around the cabin to find him standing still, gazing at two decomposed bodies in the dirt. "This is where my stepfather's sons, Kyle and Zeke, died." They were piled together against the cabin. "This is where I killed them."

"Why would you bring me here?" Oliver stared at me in the way Bruce Wayne must have stared at the man who murdered his parents.

"My stepfather would send Kyle and Zeke into the woods to hunt and beat me. This is where I proved I was the most worthy to survive the apocalypse."

"And you thought it was the best time to tell me this just after I killed a kid?"

"This is my Fortress of Solitude. Where I go when I need to recharge. Where you can come, too."

Oliver's shoulders relaxed, and a small smile emerged from his lips. "You're sharing your biggest secret with me?"

"Go inside the cabin. Cry it out. Rest. There are military meals stored here. Do what you have to do—"

"Because . . .?"

I hoped Oliver understood me. That he knew this walk was about more than just getting over his sadness.

"I found my stepfather, and you and I need to figure out just how big a threat he's become."

"Shit. That's not what I would have guessed you were going to say. Enough secrets." Oliver said. "Our lives are obviously in danger, and we deserve to know what we're up against."

He wasn't wrong. His life was in danger, as was

everyone else's.

"Before the Fall, there were men who obeyed laws only because they were forced to obey the laws." I leaned against the cabin and rested the tips of my machetes on the sod. "My stepfather was not that kind of man. He cared nothing of laws because he saw the end coming. Not that he was always like that. When he first married my mom, he was kind and gentle. But at his work in an auto body shop, a piece of metal hit him in the eye. Broke clean through his safety goggles. Blinded him in that eye.

"That day he started having visions of a dead world. He claimed that his missing eye gave him The Sight and that we needed to prepare for the coming end times. He used me to train his sons. But I watched them and picked up everything they did. From observing them, and practicing in secret, I learned to hunt, to scavenge, and to fight. My stepfather won't outright kill us. He'll wear us down first. He'll test us for weakness. Once he knows us as he knows himself, then he'll kill us."

"He wants revenge." Oliver's shoulders were relaxed, but his face was scrunched up. He didn't need me to tell him he was right. He turned toward the cabin. Before closing the door, he asked, "Could you at least bury your brothers—stepsiblings—so this place doesn't seem so morbid?"

When the door closed, I considered it. I wanted them to rot where I had killed them. They didn't deserve a proper burial. But, for Oliver, I'd place them in a shallow unmarked grave.

I took Oliver to the gibbets first, just to give him a

sense of what we were dealing with. Oliver stopped at the edge of the woods, staring at the lifeless men inside the cages. Behind me were the sounds of Oliver gagging, puking, and finally coughing up whatever was left in his stomach. I stopped near one of the cages and remembered the fellow I had seen strung up in the town. I had wanted to throw up, too.

"What the hell is this place?" Oliver asked, as he sidled up to me.

Before I could answer, the clang of a tin bucket hitting against someone's leg interrupted us. The walk sounded casual, so I guessed the fight earlier hadn't upset the routine at the resort. Meant my stepfather's people were cocky and confident.

We were too far into the bushes to see them, so we made our way through and out of the woods toward the noise. To where the resort opened into a series of cabins. Where a sports field once stood, cows grazed inside wooden fences. A few kids were milking those cows, and the slapping of the tin bucket against a leg turned out to be from another kid heading off to do her chores. As quietly as possible, we crept along the edge of the woods around the field.

Near the barn, several men started shouting. Then we heard the echo of fist on flesh. I scurried to the side of the barn, keeping low to the ground, with Oliver following. A ladder led to the roof—possibly a lookout spot. I hadn't seen any lookouts yet, but that didn't mean they weren't there. I climbed the ladder slowly and carefully. No noise came from the roof, and after peering over the top of the ladder I saw that no one was at the top. I waved for Oliver to follow, and he did.

Children of Ruin

From our vantage point, we saw a burly man being pushed to the center of another field between the barn we were on and what looked like the main house. He was blindfolded and gagged. But even with the coverings, I clearly saw bruises. A man stood on either side of him. One with a rifle and the other with a broom pole attached to the man's neck by a noose—like those mancatchers dog catchers used on vicious dogs. The rest of the colony had gathered as if watching a show.

I glanced around the yard, searching for lookout spots. The attic window on the house had no glint from the sun, so I guessed they must have removed the glass. An obvious, strategic lookout. Knowing my stepfather, I guessed his guards were most likely scattered throughout the woods, sitting in hunting seats, camouflaged so they wouldn't be easy to spot. We were just plain lucky *we* hadn't yet been spotted.

I scanned the crowd to find my stepfather, my heart beating fast. A tall man emerged with a machete in one hand. When his face became visible, and I saw the scar that replaced his eye, all I wanted to do was run away.

"Do you know what the hell is going on?" Oliver whispered to me, tugging my shoulder to get my attention.

"Not entirely," I answered in a voice meant to shush him.

My stepfather spoke, but we couldn't hear him. The crowd responded in unison with, "The One-Eyed Man is King!" As soon as their cheers ended, he stabbed the man in the chest, and cheers rose.

Oliver covered his mouth with his hands, and I worried he might be sick again. Anger. Anger and fear. That was what *I* felt. The man who'd been stabbed started to rise and claw at my stepfather. The guy holding the pole fought to keep the burly man, now a deader, from getting at anyone. My stepfather spoke more words, and three men headed down the road with the deader. I wished we were close enough to hear what my stepfather was saying.

"We need to get the hell out of here before we're caught," Oliver said with a trembling voice.

We started back into the woods, hoping no one had spotted us. I took one last glance for the lookouts, but still didn't spot any. At least now I knew where my stepfather was. I could return later without Oliver to figure out how to defeat him. How *I* could defeat him.

As we made our way to our colony, dusk was just setting in. The music was still a good half-mile away when I heard it. CDs of some band my stepfather believed "offered a good message" that my stepsiblings used to play. The lyrics rang clearer and louder the closer we got.

Once again, Big Guy and Skinny acted in a way that put us all in danger. The army brats didn't know our location, but my stepfather did. And I knew my stepfather was close, and just waiting for us to let our guard down. Playing loud music and turning the apocalypse into a party sent the message that we weren't preparing for him.

About halfway through the field, I saw Skinny sitting on the front stoop. He waved, Oliver waved back, and Skinny turned off the music. I didn't wave. Anger was boiling inside me. My colony was completely blind to the danger that we just saw of the gibbets and of the man we had just watched get executed. I needed to calm myself.

"You don't want to go in there," Skinny said with an

odd smirk when I opened my eyes and approached the stoop.

"What's going on?" I asked.

"Let's just say that Kady and Tom have realized they just might be the last quarterback and cheerleader on Earth."

I had no idea what that meant. I stepped back so I could see the roof.

"Who's on watch?"

"Uh, I am. From down here . . . No way I was going to walk through the house with them two—"

A bulky man tackled Skinny from behind. It happened so fast that Oliver and I didn't have time to react. A deader! And he had his mouth right on Skinny's neck.

I ran around them. Grabbed the burly deader by the shoulders. Yanked hard to get him off Skinny. He turned and snarled at me. He was the man my stepfather had executed. This realization startled me, giving him just enough time to lunge at me. Connor jumped and knocked him away. I drew my machete and stabbed the deader in the brainpan.

Skinny was on the ground holding his neck. He was screaming, but I didn't see any blood. He should have been covered in blood.

Just then Big Guy emerged at the door, looking rather disheveled.

"Skinny is now dead!" I growled, running to stand chest to chest with Big Guy. "And it's all your fault!"

I turned back to the others and said, "I'm the only reason any of you are alive. Without me, you would all be dead. When are you going to listen to me?"

"What's your problem?" Big Guy said through pursed

lips, puffing out his chest and glaring at me. He didn't see the deader or what had happened to Skinny. His attitude reminded me of the time in the schoolyard when the football team had ganged up on me. I remembered how he had mocked me, and how merciless he was in making sure everyone knew he was going to pound me. I remembered not being able to fight back.

"It's the end of the world. Excuse me for wanting to live a little." Big Guy turned to go back into the house.

I let the sensation in my chest build. That urge to strike back. Strike harder. *You are too weak to strike back; you need to learn pain*, my stepfather would have told me.

The next thing I knew, I was rushing the quarterback.

He was used to taking hits. He knew how to roll with a tackle, and I wasn't heavy enough to bring him down. He dug his feet into the ground and hunkered down low. This was where I wanted him. Where I had wanted him to be when I'd had to let him pound me. I stopped just short of hitting him. I jumped into the air and brought my knee smashing into his nose.

I heard Oliver shout at me as Big Guy grunted and fell back. I sidekicked him in the chest. He staggered until he landed on his back, his red face contorted as if he was shocked.

Oliver stepped between us. "Are you two crazy? We don't have enough problems?"

Skinny took his hand away from his neck. He was sobbing and breathing in heavy rasps. "He didn't bite me."

"What?" Oliver ran to examine him. "We saw him . . ."

Skinny showed us his neck and sure enough the skin wasn't broken. I left Big Guy on his back and walked to the deader. Through its open mouth, I saw just blackened gums where teeth should have been. Before or after my stepfather had killed the deader, he must have pulled out all its teeth.

"He's toying with us," I said under my breath.

"What do you mean? Who's toying with us?"

I ignored Skinny and walked toward my shelter. Connor gave a short bark, and I looked over my shoulder at the house. Connor was sitting on the stoop, his tail wagging only slightly and his head cocked.

"Come!" I shouted, and he tore through the grass to me. He stopped at my side.

Oliver was at the front door, watching. Big Guy pushed past him, holding his nose. Before Oliver disappeared inside, he said, "I'll tell them about your stepfather. About what we saw."

CHAPTER FIFTEEN

The next day, I watched from the roost as Oliver and Big Guy worked on the fence. I kept a keen eye on the woods, listened to the birds, and kept note of changes in scent as the wind brushed by me. But I also watched Oliver and Big Guy work together. I heard Kady and Skinny carrying the water jug from the lake long before they emerged from the forest, their voices making me think back to the toothless deader from the day before. Did the men who meant to kill Kady have anything to do with my stepfather? And if so, was she a part of their colony?

I took out my notebook and flipped through the pages to when I had rescued her. She was hurt. Blood was on her right shoulder. When we got to her shelter, she insisted I shower before I came inside. Was it to keep me from tracking in dirt or was there another reason? What hadn't she wanted me to see? Kady circled the house until she was with Oliver as he held posts in holes that Big Guy was securing by filling the holes with dirt.

"Hey, Ollie, can we talk?" Kady had her hands behind her back and was swaying her hips slightly.

"Ollie?" He spat the name out as if he had just tasted

rotten meat. "Facebook status: 'Cheerleader crossed the line today.' Promise you'll never call me that again, and I might say yes."

"Fine. Oliver, can we talk?" Kady said, standing up straight. I started to like Oliver even more. He was just such a straight-to-the-point guy.

I barely heard as Kady asked, "Can you teach me to fight?"

Oliver's face was not hard to read— he was both satisfied and disappointed. Knowing him now as I did, I guessed his satisfaction came from Kady wanting to be more than the cheerleader who got what she wanted by flirting. But, no doubt, that the world had become a place where violence seemed the right answer to every question still disappointed him.

"Why not ask Tom?"

"I did. But I don't think he takes me seriously enough. You're more patient, too. I'm tired of being a clichéd cheerleader, I want to be more of a warrior like Katniss."

Oliver reached out and felt her bicep. "All that water you've been carrying from the lake has given you some good muscle. Bet all those cheers you do mean you have strong legs." He paused for about five seconds before nodding. "Tomorrow I'll switch my free time with Blake so you and I can train. I'll be patient, but I'm not going easy on you."

"Thanks," Kady said as she leaned over and kissed his cheek. I found myself turning red, and just as I looked away Oliver caught me watching.

"Hey, General!" Oliver had an *I know you were watching me* tone to his voice. "We scavenging today?"

Inside the house, Skinny filled the filter with lake water.

Big Guy still dug holes for posts, sweating under the hot sun. I didn't want to admit I was watching Oliver and Kady, or that watching them together made me . . . jealous.

Why would it make me jealous?

This could be the perfect timing to find out what Kady hadn't said about her family. My stepfather had never known about her place, or all the things worth scavenging: the generator, the other bike armor, and all the canned goods inside the shelter. Possibly more inside the house. Without a truck, we could get only the canned goods home, but we needed the extra food.

"Yeah. We'll head to Kady's. This time, for her supplies," I shouted down to Oliver.

"I'll come. I can get my clothes and make-up," Kady shouted back at me.

"No. We're going only for food and necessities."

"My make-up is a necessity!"

It surprised me that she didn't stomp her foot. Still, I tried to remember when Oliver had talked to me about hobbies. About feeling normal. I understood that what she asked wasn't really about make-up. It was about feeling like the whole world hadn't just collapsed—her make-up was my comics. Oliver looked up at me with that same look he had when he'd first explained hobbies to me, and I nodded to him to let him know that I got the message.

"Kady," Oliver said, "I promise I'll get your stuff if you write down what you need."

"Thanks," she said. And this time when she kissed his cheek she kept an eye on me.

Oliver walked a few paces behind me and Connor, with

his crossbow loaded. He'd been different since killing the little girl we'd found on the farm. . . quiet. Almost solemn. After an hour had passed, we emerged from the woods into the meadow where Kady's house was. Oliver nearly walked by me, but I held out my arm and stopped him short.

"What?"

I pointed to one of the basement windows, and he saw the broken glass. I stuck along the tree line so I could see the shed. Sure enough, the door was open. Not much chance of us finding anything left of value in the house.

"Good thing Kady came to stay with us," Oliver said, as he relaxed his crossbow for the first time since we'd been walking. Seemed off to me that he'd relax his weapon now, just when danger presented itself.

"They could still be here." I drew my machetes. "Stay close to me."

I ran, crouched, across the lawn toward the back of the house. Connor was right on my heels. It was a big two-story house, plus attic, no doubt with plenty of rooms to hide in. Having seen what Kady was like in my colony, I imagined my stepfather's men had caught her without a struggle while she was sunbathing. I didn't understand why they hadn't looted her shelter—or, if it was locked, why they hadn't forced her to open it. More and more evidence was pointing to a connection between Kady and my stepfather's colony.

A crash from inside the house stopped us in our tracks. Oliver and Connor watched me, as if waiting for me to move. Oliver readied his crossbow. Connor only sniffed the air, so it wasn't deaders. If it had been, Connor would have been barking and growling and backing away.

"Could be squatters. Could be the army brats. Could be the ones who murdered the Jeffersons."

Oliver nodded. What I didn't think he understood was that we most likely had to kill whomever we found inside. Kady's home held valuable information, especially if her dad, as a scientist, knew the virus was coming. He might have left behind papers or a hint as to where he might have disappeared to. And while Oliver may have had it in him to kill deaders, I was sure he didn't have it in him to kill the living.

"Stay here. I want to check things out first."

I left Oliver and crept around the house with Connor beside me, matching my speed. I neared the front of the house. Heavy steps running down the front stoop, followed by lighter steps. Two people were outside. I steeled myself to kill them. I wished Oliver wasn't with me. That he wouldn't see how easily I fit into a world that scared him. Even before I peered around the house to get a full view of the front yard, I heard a man speaking.

"Open up your glove more, and wait until you feel the ball before you close your hand."

Peering around the house, I saw an old guy in his forties tossing a baseball to a kid no more than six, a year older than my sister. They were throwing the ball overhanded, back and forth. The boy smiled and laughed whenever he missed and had to chase after it. What a strange sight seeing them playing a game instead of training for survival. I tried to imagine my stepfather throwing a ball to me. That nearly made me laugh.

My attention was so focused on the father and son that I didn't notice Connor whimpering and scurrying backward. I didn't know where the deader had come from, but he suddenly rushed the boy, whose laughter then turned to screams. The dad shouted, but the deader was nearly on top of the child. I rushed out, but the dad was between his son and me. The deader grabbed the boy, lifting him toward its open jaw. The monster was about to chomp the boy when a bolt slammed through its head. Oliver had shot it from behind. The dad slowly looked over his shoulder at me with my two machetes. Then back at Oliver with his crossbow.

"Go to your son," I told him.

The child was shaking, with a dark spot growing below his waist. A pool of liquid ran out the bottom of his pants. His eyes bore into me as he pushed his cheek deep into his father's chest. I knew I'd never have been able to kill them. I thought of when my mom had first married my stepfather, of his two sons, both older than me, and of how they had looked like miniature versions of him.

"This is not a discussion," my stepfather had said to my mom. His voice giving me chills for the first time. "I have a place out in the woods. When the end falls, we'll be safe." He had paused to stare at me. His eyes boring into me and his words like punches to my soul. "I'll make us strong."

My mom never wrapped her arms around me again. I never buried my face deep into her chest again. No one ever made me feel safe again. I broke from that memory as Oliver put his hand on my shoulder. He glanced again at my machetes, still drawn, and motioned with his head that I should sheathe them.

"What do you want?" the father asked us just as the mother burst through the front door. She pointed a pistol at us, shaking so badly that she was just as likely to hit her husband or son as us.

"We just saved you." Oliver held up his hands to surrender.

I didn't follow his example.

"But you came to scavenge, didn't you?"

"This house belongs to a friend of ours," Oliver said slowly, as though carefully choosing his words. I studied the mom, waiting for an opportunity to get that gun away from her.

"Nobody owns anything anymore," the dad said, "'cept by force."

"Put your weapons down," the mom warned us, her voice shaking more than the gun, "and get on your knees!"

"We saved your son!" Oliver shouted back, as his crossbow hit the dirt. He dropped to his knees, but I stayed standing.

"You, too!" the mom screamed.

"No." I pointed the tips of my machetes toward the dad and kid. "Think you can shoot me, hit me, before I run them through?"

I don't know whose face grew redder or whose expression looked more horrified, the mom's or Oliver's.

"I'll—I'll shoot you from here!"

"Miss, and you kill your husband and son."

Spit flew from the mom's mouth in place of words. Oliver slowly rose to his feet and loaded a bolt in his crossbow. Oliver had no compassion in his voice, just like when he'd first seen all the dead soldiers around my house. "All we want is to take a look around for some of our friend's stuff."

"Martha! No!" the dad shouted as the mom lowered her gun.

"There ain't nothing left in here. What little food we found, we ate."

"We're looking for papers." I didn't need to look at Oliver to know that was not what he had expected to me to say.

"What papers we found, we burned." The dad said this too quickly. "For cooking. For heat."

Stalemate. The mom held the gun at her side. The dad gripped his son. Oliver had a loaded crossbow. And me, armed with my machetes. Even after we'd saved their lives, they had zero interest in helping us. What it came down to was simple—either we kill this family, or we walk away with nothing.

"Fine. We're leaving." Oliver made the decision quickly. As though worried it wouldn't be the one I'd make. We kept our weapons ready, and Connor kept growling. The mom raised her gun and kept it pointed at us until we were in the bushes.

"Where is Kady's shelter?" Oliver asked.

"Once it's dark, it may be near impossible to see. It'll also be impossible to get Connor in and out of it. Was that your plan? To wait until dark and sneak to the shelter?"

He mouthed yes, his cheeks showing a little embarrassment. After a pause, he said, "I don't want to kill them." Oliver knew these people wanted to kill us. And they were squatting in Kady's home. He knew the old rules didn't matter, and that the new rule, the only rule, was that might won. "What do we do, General?"

"Your plan is good. We sleep in Kady's shelter. Connor stays outside. The deaders aren't interested in him, and he needs to learn to guard and wait. We don't need to kill this family."

Oliver patted my back, and I wondered if that was meant as a sort of hug.

We waited for the darkness to come before we made our way to the shelter. Candle lights flickered in the house, and I assumed the family was staying awake on watch in case we returned. No beams of light shone from the windows, so maybe they didn't have flashlights. If we had chosen to kill them, it wouldn't have been hard to do right then.

Connor followed close on our heels. I paid him extra attention in case he smelled deaders. We managed to locate the hatch. I opened it with Kady's combo. Oliver climbed in first, and as I started down the ladder, Connor circled to find a way inside.

"Stay here," I told him, and he whimpered as he licked my face. With his head down he wagged his tail slowly. "Guard the hatch. Stay."

I closed the lid and, until the seal locked, heard Connor whimpering and clawing at the hatch. Inside, I felt my way along the wall until I found the switches. The lights and fans came alive. Oliver bumped my shoulder to pass me.

"This is where Kady was living? No wonder she hates our colony so much. I'd be a total bitch if I had to leave here."

"There's a shower and beds we can sleep in. I'll make us dinner if you want to wash up."

"We are going to talk about why you asked about papers," Oliver said just before he headed for the washroom. I nodded and started searching the cupboards. There was enough canned food to last for months, and no reason we couldn't store it here for safekeeping. We'd have to sneak past the family living in Kady's home, but I had a feeling the army brats would take care of them for us, eventually.

The shower turned on just as I opened a tin of stew. I found three bowls—one for Connor—and two spoons. Other than luxuries and food, it didn't seem as if Kady's father had planned for anything. No weapons, no exercise equipment, not even surveillance.

While Oliver was in the shower, I got the idea that he might like fresh, clean clothes. I didn't want to make him wear Kady's brother's loser clothes, but thought he might like me to wash his. Doing something that might make him happy made me smile.

I wandered over to the bathroom and listened at the door. The water was going, and he was taking extra long with it. Didn't blame him, as it might be his last shower. I gently turned the knob and slowly opened the door so he wouldn't hear me. The clothes were on the floor. I reached in and grabbed them. His trousers, gitch, shirt, socks, and what looked like a black rubber back brace. I managed to get them out and into the washer without him knowing. I didn't throw the back brace in, since I wasn't sure it could be washed. I wondered what was wrong with his back.

"Uh, hey General, where's my clothes?" Oliver yelled from the bathroom, after he'd finished.

I rushed back to the kitchen and searched for the can opener. "I threw them in the wash. Just throw a towel around your waist."

There was a pause. Not a wrapping-a-towel-around-the-waist-before-emerging-type pause, but a really long uncertain-what-to-do pause before he said in a cracked voice, "Can't."

"What? Why? Just get out here." I found the can opener and started opening the can.

"Can you please just bring me back my clothes?"

I stopped what I was doing. Ridiculous. "What's your problem?"

Again, a silence that lasted too long. I started walking toward the shower and stopped just short of the door. I could have just gotten him clothes from Kady's brother's closet, but that just seemed so strange that I didn't want to.

Instead, I reached for the door handle, but it turned before I had a chance to grab it. The door opened slowly. Oliver stood behind it with a towel wrapped around him up past his chest. Before I could ask what he was doing, I saw the towel covered bumps on his chest that had been squished down by the brace. We still didn't speak, and the silence was getting more uncomfortable. His lower lip was trembling, and his eyes were as red as his cheeks. Or rather, *her* cheeks.

"My name is Olive, not Oliver—"

"You don't have a sister, do you?"

Tears slowly fell from her eyes. Some caught on her cheeks, and some landed on the floor. Now I understood the story Oliver had told me. There was no sister. After the men had beaten him up, he died as a girl and woke as a boy. I had nothing in my experiences to draw on to know how to fix this. I reached out and hugged her. At first Oliver was rigid and shaking. She didn't hold me back, and it was awkward. I considered letting go, but instead I held her tighter. Slowly, she wrapped her arms around me and buried her face in my shoulder.

"This is awkward," she said. "Can you take a shower

while I finish making dinner?"

"I want to help you feel better."

Oliver let me go, and I released my hold on her. She cupped my chin in her hand and smiled. "Facebook status: 'Ethan needs to take a shower and stop stinking up the place.'" Then she said in a less snarky tone, "That'll make me feel better."

After a quick shower, I found Oliver in the living room dressed in a baggy T-shirt and sweatpants. I was in a towel. I threw my clothes into the washer to begin the cycle.

"What's the plan, General?" Oliver said, as if nothing had changed.

"I don't care that you're a girl," I told her. "I won't tell anyone."

"I know. It's just . . ."

"You're not Olive anymore?"

"Like you're not the boy who was hunted by your stepbrothers."

Sorry is what my mom had whispered the night before my stepfather had first taken me into the woods. "If you can run away tomorrow, do it. Never come back," was the last thing she had ever said to me. Maybe my mom saw herself disappearing into a shell. Or maybe she hoped for strength in me that she never possessed. I had believed, at the time, that she had made me weak. That she had the opinion of me as not worthy to sit at my stepfather's table.

And as Oliver retreated to the bedroom, I hoped things hadn't changed like that between us.

CHAPTER SIXTEEN

We used my mirror trick to safely get out of the shelter the next morning. The sun cast only enough light for us to see objects as silhouettes, but I could still tell that it was safe. When I climbed from the hatch, Connor ran to me, panting, his tail wagging against the grass. I had a bowl of stew for Connor, and he lapped it up quickly. For all I knew, that stew could have been dog food labeled as human food. Oliver passed me up a rucksack filled with cans. I grunted as I lifted it up and onto the ground. After she'd handed me up a second rucksack, she climbed out.

"Wait, is there another bag down there?" I called to her.

"Yeah, but don't you think two bags will be plenty heavy?"

"Get a third."

Oliver stood there, just staring at me. After raising her eyebrows and breathing heavily through pursed lips, she did as I asked. I knew it was a time waster, but I just felt as though it was needed. Connor watched around me, sniffing the air as if for scents stronger than the dew.

Oliver finally handed me up a third cloth grocery bag.

"All I could find," she said, as she came up the ladder.

"Wait a sec," I told her. I grabbed the grocery bag and ran toward the house. Connor watched me before tearing through the grass after me. Oliver stayed with the two rucksacks.

I scurried around to the front door of the house, knowing these people were just as likely to shoot me as they were to greet me. Probably more likely to shoot me. I considered why I was leaving the food there; did I want to make them allies, or just keep their kid from starving? Superheroes followed a code to protect the weak, which was what made my stepfather the supervillain—that he hurt the weak. I lay the bag down at their front door, and then I started off. They didn't need to know the food had come from me. I did this because it was right. But as I stepped onto the last stair of their stoop, the front door opened. I looked over my shoulder. The mom, gun in hand, stared from me to the food and back again.

"Why? We tried to kill you."

"Each time we come back for more, we'll leave you a bag. One day, we may come with a truck. You have my word that we'll leave the house to you."

With Connor at my heels, I turned to leave just as the woman grabbed the bag and took it inside. If she rationed the food out, maybe she'd have a month of meals. Somehow I doubted she'd run out of food before the army brats found them and ended them. This wasn't a "see you later"; it was a "goodbye forever." One day we'd return and I'd be able to look through the house for those papers, and I wouldn't have to lay a hand on anyone inside.

I returned to Oliver and grabbed a rucksack. She punched my shoulder and gave me a big smile. "You always surprise me," she said, taking the second rucksack.

I watched after her as she headed toward the woods. I didn't look down at her knowing what I knew about her, just as she never looked down at me no matter what she learned about me.

We walked in the middle of the road that entered the compound. We wanted to be visible so no one would think we were intruders and snipe at us. Connor was by my side. My arms were aching from carrying the heavy rucksack—no doubt Oliver, who wasn't nearly as brawny as me, ached even worse. We didn't speak the whole way back, just exchanged these weird glances where Oliver would smile at me.

Kady waved from the roost and Oliver waved back. Big and Skinny were hoisting a pole on the roost—probably for the wind turbine Skinny had been researching. The fence posts, all in place, just needed wire to finish them. No more dead bodies littered the ground, and a nice stockpile of firewood sat by the shed. Next I saw what they probably hoped I wouldn't. The door to the shed was open. The lock broken. I stopped cold in my tracks.

"What?" Oliver asked, as she took a few more steps before stopping.

"They opened the shed. You were never to open the shed!" I listened to the tone of my words. Calm. No anger. Like how I imagined Uncle Ben would have sounded when Peter had started blowing off his chores and refused to take his Spider-Man power seriously. Disappointment. The trust we had built. The goodwill I had experienced. All gone. Washed away.

Children of Ruin

I dropped my sack of cans nearly on top of Connor, who scampered away, and I collapsed to the ground as if a force pulled me to my knees.

"Oh, god. What did they do?" Oliver whispered, and hurried toward the house.

Long before Oliver got there, Skinny dashed from the front door with Big Guy close behind him. They talked, and I watched, frozen, as their lips moved. Skinny, shaking his head, pointed at the shed. *They know. Now they know.*

Skinny, Big Guy, and Oliver all started toward me. I couldn't help but see them walking in slow motion as pressure built in my head. I rocked, hoping that just maybe the movement would jar loose the emotions I could not name or control. *Go in the shed,* I heard my stepfather tell me. *You will understand pain. You will become a man in that shed.*

"I didn't know," Skinny said, as he leaned onto one knee so he was face-to-face with me.

"We wondered if there'd be tools in there," Big Guy said from behind Skinny.

Oliver was walking to the shed. Where she'd see it. Where she'd see just how I became what I am. The chair. The chains. The leather strap. The darkness inside. Just like the darkness within me.

I couldn't hear Oliver speak, but when she looked inside the open door and her hand covered her mouth, I knew she'd whispered, "Oh, dear god." Whatever progress I'd made with my colony was gone. I would be alone again. They would never stay with a boy as broken as me. A villain playing the hero. *Pretending.*

Skinny put a hand on my shoulder. His stillness made me aware of my shaking. "No one will ever do this to you again," he said.

Hearing words that didn't match what I expected him to say seemed weird. *Freak! Weirdo! Get in that shed!* That's what I waited for—but those words weren't coming from any of them.

"Blake and I talked it over," Big Guy said. "We want to chop down that shed and burn it. It shouldn't be there. It never should have been there."

Oliver rushed to me with a blanket that she must have gotten from the house. She wrapped me in it tightly as I rocked. "Bring him Connor," she said.

And Connor was in front of me, his nose on my nose. He made me feel calmer, and as the rush in my head began to subside, I could hear what they were saying. Hear the words for what was said, and not for what I feared.

"No one will ever do this to you again."

"We'll burn the shed. Get rid of it."

"You're with family now."

The afternoon was filled with the noise of hammer and ax on wood. I wanted to be a part of it, to help with the destruction of what my stepfather had once called my "training shed." But Oliver decided it would be better if I stayed away. That bringing back memories might be worse than the cathartic destruction of my nightmare.

As I stood at the riverbed, Connor at my feet and Oliver treading water, I still couldn't completely agree with her.

"Kady is watching for intruders, and Blake will come get us when they're finished. Why don't you just swim?"

"I can't," I said flatly, concentrating on Connor's panting and not on the breaking wood.

"You could if you wanted to. Nothing is stopping you—"

"No, I can't." The finality in my tone stopped Oliver from finishing her sentence. No one had ever taught me to swim. It wasn't seen as something important, like something I would need to know. Kyle and Zeke had learned, but they were supposed to survive the coming end of days.

Oliver swam back to shore and walked out from the water. Even though this spot was completely secret from everyone, Oliver stayed in her shirt and shorts. Her shirt was wet and tight against her skin, and I could tell she was a girl.

She walked up to me and took my hand. That thing passed through me when her fingers touched mine. That spark that tingled in my fingers and grew until it consumed my entire body. Without words, she pulled me toward the water. I pulled back, but not because I didn't want to go with her.

"I still have my clothes on. My machetes and armor."

She cocked her head slightly, and I noticed Connor mimic her. Oliver reached out to my chest and unhooked my straps. The machetes fell to the ground with a clang. She then unclasped my shoulder straps, removing my body armor. I started to feel uneasy, vulnerable to attack, but I couldn't bring myself to stop her. When she was this close, even as she was pulling off my T-shirt, a shiver passed through me as though her touch returned a part of me that had been missing.

Oliver turned my back to her by gently pushing my shoulders. Her fingers traced the scars that went from between my shoulder blades all the way to the small of my back. It didn't tickle as it would have had she been my sister. She turned me back to face her.

"You can decide if you want to get in the water with your pants or shorts."

I kicked off my pants and followed her into the river. As my feet submerged, a brown pool formed around them. Not from the riverbed, but from me. I stopped waist deep and just watched as the dirt washed away. Goose bumps riddled my flesh, and my muscles tensed from the cold water. It was weird.

"It's easier if you just jump right in," Oliver said, as she waded in chest deep.

I took her advice and dove in up to my shoulders. My chest tightened and my breathing got raspy. The water washed away the rest of the grime from my skin. A small amount got in my mouth. I splashed in the water to get closer to shore, but a pull carried me toward the center of the river. It wasn't strong, but it was stronger than I was.

"I've got you." And Oliver was there, her arms under mine, and she was kicking at the water and drifting me back toward shore. Again, her touch on my skin was like a spark that zapped away the fear and worry that the water had given me.

Oliver and I spent the rest of the day in the water, her teaching me a new skill while the three others destroyed the last grasp my stepfather had on me. For the first time, I felt surrounded by family. I understood what it meant to have a family. And no one would ever take that from me. Or so I wanted to believe.

CHAPTER SEVENTEEN

Kady's screech caught my attention as I watched the surrounding forest from the roost. Oliver had thrown her over her shoulder, and because we had no mats, Kady landed hard on the grass. I thought about what it must have been like for Oliver when she was attacked by the men posing as telephone repair guys—back when we all figured the world still made sense. I was betting she could have fought her way out, if she'd had it in her mentally. Oliver kept pushing Kady so she collapsed to the ground on her back every time she tried to get back up.

"Hey! That hurts!" Kady protested loudly.

I couldn't hear Oliver, but I knew she was telling Kady that she needed to be ready. To take any chance to win. Oliver and I thought a lot alike, and that's how I would have trained Kady. My attention snapped back into focus when I heard footfalls on the stairs.

"I need a welding tool," Skinny said, without wasting time on any other kind of small talk. I was starting to respect him now that he asked for what he wanted rather than passive-aggressively hinting at what he would perhaps like me to get him.

"Why?"

"Because we can get this wind generator going with the bike gears you brought back, but I need to cut parts so they fit. And I need to anchor a car alternator to something."

I considered that for a moment as Kady grunted loudly and *hoof*ed at the air. "Lots of cars to scavenge in town."

Skinny nodded and wrung his hands. He looked up at the pole he and Big Guy had hoisted up. He tapped it so that it rang. I stared down at the pile of rubble that had once been the shed. I could still see traces of cuffs and chains, and beating rods glinting in the sunlight. Connor sat beside me, his focus on Oliver as she trained Kady in self-defense. Oliver commanded her: "Strike harder!"; "Go for the crotch!"; "Poke the eyes!" It wasn't the same as when I had snuck onto the roost to watch my stepfather train his sons. Or when I had crept from my house long before twilight to practice in secret.

"You and Big Guy want to use some of the shed to make this turbine, don't you?"

Skinny didn't answer straight away, and I knew I was in for more than just a light convo about crafting some new invention. I considered telling him to either speak his mind or get on with his day. But pushing him wasn't going to make him stronger. If he was going to survive, he needed to get over his cowardice.

"Could you not call him that?" His voice was raspy, and he paused to take a long puff of his asthma meds. The puffer didn't make the *pshhhh* sound that it normally made. "And don't call me Skinny no more, either. I have a name, and so does Tom. It really pisses us off when you call down to us like that."

I nodded. His outburst meant we had a better chance of surviving, that his desire to live outweighed his fear of getting killed. And after everything that had happened, I couldn't doubt his sincerity in wanting to mend fences. "Sorry. I'll call you Blake from now on."

"Y'know, I get that this world isn't what it once was. I finally get it. Really. More now than I did before. But I'm not who I used to be, either."

"Yeah, sure." Just as my words left my lips, I spotted an extended flatbed truck pulling into our driveway. A tarp covered the flatbed, hiding what could be anything—even people. I could barely make out two people in the cab, and neither appeared armed. Blake turned to where I was looking and went all wide eyed again. Short window of bravado. He still didn't have it in him to deal with these intruders if they turned out to be violent.

Tom ran between the house and truck and Oliver followed him. Kady rushed into the house. I aimed the rifle at the flatbed's bumper—all I wanted was for it not to come closer. I pulled the trigger. A *bang*! Then sparks flew from the truck. I'd hit it dead on. The driver slammed on the brakes. Kady emerged onto the roost. After that, nothing happened. It must have been seconds, but it felt like minutes. Finally, the two strangers reached out the windows, their palms open.

"We've come to trade!" the driver yelled.

Oliver looked up at me, and I nodded to her. "Check how legit these guys are," I called down. Behind me, Blake used his empty puffer, fear dripping from his every rasp. Kady, wide eyed, grabbed the rifle from me. I was hopeful these guys were for real, no doubt we all were, but if they weren't, we'd have to react severely.

Oliver stood near enough to talk with them, but didn't speak loud enough for me to hear. A man and woman exited the vehicle and stood between Oliver and Tom, who was gripping the sledgehammer he had been using to drive posts into the ground. I wanted to know if the tarp covered supplies to trade or people hiding to fight? Just as the question formed in my head, Oliver pointed at the tarp.

"You need to get down there," Kady said, her shaking hands pointing the rifle at the truck.

"Can you?" I asked her.

She scrunched up her face and shrugged. Blake shook his head no.

"Can you shoot these people if they try to take what isn't theirs? They'll kill us. They'll kill *you*."

"I'll try," Kady said.

Did she understand that her training with Oliver was about preparing to deal with invaders? Kady stared at me while I watched Oliver get nearer the truck. I turned away for a second when Blake slowly reached for another rifle. As he wrapped his fingers around it, he moved to Kady's side. A big part of me didn't believe they'd do it—but I had to trust them. I couldn't be in two places at once, and I needed to be down below more than I needed to be a sniper up there. Blake rested the barrel on the railing, pointing the sight at the strangers. Kady did the same with her rifle. Both crouched on one knee and put their eyes to the scopes.

I told them, "Choose one person. The most visible, and concentrate on that one. If you're indecisive about who to shoot, you will give them time to get cover. Hopefully, it won't come to that."

Children of Ruin

I didn't give Blake or Kady time to think about their answer. Without a choice, I turned and left the roost. If I'd been alone, maybe I would have just killed these strangers. Maybe I would have traded with them. Rushing through the house to get outside, I knew only that the scared boy who ran helpless from his stepbrothers no longer existed inside me. *My colony made me better*, I admitted to myself. As I left the house, I heard the tail end of what Oliver was saying. ". . . need a generator. That's what would be useful."

The driver nodded his head. "No worries. We got just what you need."

What happened next was a blur. A man appeared from beneath the tarp, aiming a rifle. It flashed fire by the time I noticed the glint of steel. A scream. Two more shots. One splattered blood in the roost. The other sent Oliver flying to the ground. I froze as two of my colony got shot. The driver and passenger both reached into their jackets. The guy in the flatbed moved his rifle, but it got caught in the tarp. Tom rushed in first. Adrenaline or instinct—or fear—drove him to react where I had suddenly frozen.

My eyes slowly moved to Oliver's dead body. That's when my adrenaline took over. As if in slow motion, the driver and passenger pulled out pistols. Tom smashed his entire body into the passenger, slamming her against the truck so hard the guy in the back collapsed with the crash. I ran, pulling my machetes free. A race against knife and pistol. Just as the driver brought his gun up, I lopped his hands clean off. He screamed and went down.

Tom crouched over the woman he'd tackled, pulling his bloodstained hammer off her smashed head. Tom gritted his teeth, sputtering saliva freely from his mouth as he screamed. The shooter, the one who had killed two of my people, now cowered in the back of the truck.

The driver stayed flat on his ass, staring at the stumps where his hands had once been. Blood spattered him in the face, and he moaned softly. I slapped Tom with the dull side of my machete to get his attention. I then gestured to the tarp, reminding him we were not finished.

You are defined by moments, my stepfather's voice reminded me. I had to agree. In every book I'd read, every comic I'd pored over, characters were weak until that one defining moment where the reality of the situation could no longer escape them. For Tom, the apocalypse had just become real. It changed from a twenty-four-seven parent-free party to the dangerous Darwinian competition of my upbringing.

Tom moved faster than I'd ever seen him move. With a loud grunt, he grabbed the tarp and tore it from the truck bed. When it ripped, it echoed. I moved in when I saw the lone gunman swinging his rifle at my last fighter. Tom didn't even take a pause as he reached out, grabbed the muzzle, and yanked so hard the guy stumbled forward and fell from the truck. The rifle blasted and dirt exploded between Tom and me. The shooter landed on the ground. A loud *crack* followed as he hit his shoulder. Tom hoisted him against the truck, pressing his forearm against the man's neck.

I didn't see generators, or food, or clothes for trade. The flatbed was empty—all we had traded were lives— some of theirs for some of ours. I looked back over my shoulder at Oliver lying still on the ground. Some of Tom's madness seeped into me. I pressed the tip of my machete against the man's face.

"Are there more of you?"

"Yes," he spat while gasping for breath. I did nothing to stop Big Guy from choking him.

"Where?" I pressed my blade harder so that blood dripped from his cheek.

"The One-Eyed Man is king!" the man said, and suddenly my chest felt as though it had caved in. I stumbled back, tripping over my own feet and falling butt first to the ground. Somewhere in my consciousness I heard the last gargles of the man as Tom choked him to death.

"Stepfather, this does not make us even," I said, as close to a whisper as my anger would allow.

"What the hell are you talking about?" Tom shouted, still not letting the shooter go.

"He's still alive!" Kady, now kneeling over Oliver, shouted from behind us. Blood covered Kady's hands as she pressed down on Oliver's shoulder.

The blood splatter over Kady's face told me Skinny was dead.

Tom ran inside the house, and I ran to Oliver. Her chest rose with her fast, raspy breaths, but at least she was breathing. I kneeled beside her, edging Kady out of the way. I felt around and discovered a hole in the front of her shoulder and another out the back. The bullet had gone clean through, and blood ran from the wound.

"Get the first aid kit," I told Kady. "NOW!"

Kady and Tom both ran for the house. I tore Oliver's shirt off her shoulder. She had her back brace wrapped around her chest so she'd look like a boy. When I tried to remove it, she weakly grabbed my hands and shook her head for me to stop.

"No one will know, I promise," I whispered to her.

She held my hands, and her grip weakened. She nodded, and tears started from her eyes. My tears fell too, landing on her cheek and running with hers down her muddied face. I couldn't lose her. I just couldn't lose her. Kady rushed back to me without Tom. I could hear him up in the roost, crying and shouting and banging the rails. I took the first aid kit from Kady.

"Go back to Tom. He needs you more than I do."

Kady kissed Oliver's forehead and ran back to the house.

I had nothing to disinfect Oliver's wound, but I had to sew the holes shut—front and back. Hopefully two holes meant no pieces of the bullet were left behind. I fished in the kit for silk thread and a needle. Ignoring the blood that poured out, and that there was no way to sanitize the needle, I pushed under her armpit to slow the bleeding and sewed her wounds. Then I finished with a bandage I made from Celox gauze and the remainder of our tape. This was not good. We needed penicillin in case she got an infection.

"Did anyone die?" Oliver asked, between sobs.

"Don't worry about it," I said. I may as well have just told her yes, because she knew me well enough to know that was what I meant. I gently squeezed Oliver's hand, and she weakly squeezed mine back. She attempted a smile, but as her eyes opened more tears ran out.

Six feet long, two feet wide, and eight feet deep. That's how much I dug. Oliver and Kady were crying openly. Tears dripped unchecked down their cheeks, as they leaned heavily against one another. After I had climbed out from the hole, Big Guy threw Skinny inside it. Skinny was smart—he'd built our water filtration system and had figured out how to make a wind turbine. Who knows what else he would have been capable of achieving? Together, Big Guy and I started burying him. Big Guy breathed hard, but not one tear fell from his eyes.

"Maybe someone should say something?" Oliver said softly. "Tom? You knew him best."

Big Guy shook his head no, his face contorting. He made a sputtering sound as tears rolled from his eyes and spit from his lips.

"Okay, I'll do it," Oliver said. "Blake was a thinker. He was always trying to fix things, and build things, and to make our lives easier. When I first met him on the credit union roof, he attempted to seem tough. He wasn't. He was a gentle kid not ready for the deaders—or for war."

"War?" Kady coughed out.

Oliver's eyes turned dark. She stopped crying. Though she stared intently at the grave, I could see that in her mind she was far off somewhere else. Oliver had changed.

"Yeah, war. We need to start preparing for the inevitable: people like this will attack again. We can't ever feel safe—not ever—or we're as good as dead."

I would have rejoiced at hearing Oliver's words when we first started scavenging together, but now they made me sad. The apocalypse was not a party. No time for games or joy. This was now the apocalypse I had been hoping for all along. And I regretted that it had come.

"Oliver, I—"

Oliver suddenly fell to her knees and retched. By her coughs and glossy eyes, I knew infection was setting into her wound faster than normal. And she knew it, too. Whatever the apocalypse had done to make the dead rise, now made the living get sick faster.

"We need antibiotics, fast," I said.

"Sure. No, prob. I'll just head down to the local pharmacy—"

I shot Big Guy a glare that cut his words short. "I'm stating a FACT, not an OPINION."

"Oh my god, I'm going to die before you two figure this out," Oliver mumbled as she opened her eyes again. She wrapped her arms around my neck and I lifted her.

"Could you two get along long enough to help me?" she asked.

I nodded. Big Guy nodded. For her, I'd do my best to try.

CHAPTER EIGHTEEN

Over the next couple of days, our quiet homestead was far from peaceful. As I stood on the roof, I tried not to think of Oliver lying in bed unable to keep down whatever we fed her. A part of me wished we hadn't killed those men. A part of me wished I still had the shed. All of me wished I could take those men into that shed to get information from them the way my stepfather had gotten information from me.

"Hey," Big Guy said as he came up the stairs, quiet-like, "I think I know where we can get penicillin."

"Penicillin or revenge?" I asked him. I knew he was thinking the same as what I'd been thinking ever since Oliver got sick.

"Do they need to be exclusive of each other? You can't tell me you don't want a little revenge, too." Tom paused, possibly to let me have a word if I wanted. "We tell Oliver and Kady we're going to get rid of the rubble, and we ditch the truck. Who needs that reminder here? Then we go find this One-Eyed King and figure out how we can end him."

His words were powerful, but I questioned just how mentally ready he was for what he'd have to do. My stepfather was no amateur survivalist—he had trained in war and death. He knew how to psychologically break us, and to make us act or react without properly thinking things through. He expected us to retaliate.

If my stepfather had Evergreen Fishing Resort on the northeast side of Loon Lake Road, and the brats had been to Clinton as well as up and down our roads, the army brats must have set up camp south toward Cache Creek. They could be farther north of Clinton, but the resources south made more sense for an army outpost. And they must have somehow taken over an outpost—how else would they have gotten the weapons they had?

Then a crazy idea came to me. I remembered a book I had read, *Watership Down*, about these rabbits who start a new colony only to discover they need more rabbits. They also find another colony where some of the rabbits want to escape their crazy leader. Maybe it could be that way with us and the army brats. We could defeat my stepfather if we aligned ourselves with his enemy. While I didn't completely trust that Timothy wasn't a nutcase, he certainly had to be more reasonable than my stepfather.

"No, we aren't ready to fight the One-Eyed King. But there's a group with proper numbers and guns who might be ready. Maybe we can convince them to join us. Even just some of them."

Kady's footsteps on the ladder made me wonder if she had heard us. I was so lost in my mind that I hadn't even noticed where she was.

"Who's paying attention in the roost?" Kady asked, her tone half mocking me. But I knew she was also serious. By what the men in the truck had said, they were with my stepfather, and that meant he had attempted to kill us. To kill me. And knowing Kady, in her mind, to kill her.

"Sorry," I said back to Kady. I really didn't know what else to say. Big Guy and I hadn't had a chance to make a plan, or come up with a lie about where we were going. I waited for her to say something else. She looked as if she were ready to say something, but she just stared at me.

"You two are going after whoever was behind this, aren't you?" Kady said quietly, her voice shaking. "Kill him. Do it for Blake, and do it for all of us. Don't be merciful. Just don't."

"Well, are we?" Big Guy asked.

I nodded and walked past them to give Kady and Big Guy a moment together before we left. I went to Oliver's room, closing the door behind me.

"That's the patter of steps of a man trying not to tell me he's off to get revenge," Oliver said, shivering beneath her comforter. I sat on the edge of the bed, kicked off my shoes, and lay beside her. It made me think back to just a few weeks earlier when she and I were at the Jeffersons' homestead and we slept in the same bed for the first time. I didn't want to admit it then, but I'd been comforted by her presence. As I wondered if she was still comforted by mine, Oliver rested her head on my shoulder and took my hand in hers.

"Do you remember the army brats?" I asked.

"The guys who shot and killed the farmer's wife? How could I forget them?" Her tone told me she knew where I was going with this, and just how stupid an idea it was she thought it was.

"They might have medicine. And some of them may want to help us." I sat up and moved to the edge of her bed, keeping her hand in mine. Her skin was calloused but clammy from fever. Time was running out, but if this was going to be the last time I saw her . . . Just as I opened my mouth to speak, Oliver quickly sat up and kissed my cheek.

"Someone could walk in, y'know," I reminded her.

"I know. I don't think I care. Life is too short."

Oliver stopped rambling. I stared at her, waiting for her to say something. I didn't know what to say. When she leaned in and pressed her lips on mine, I knew she hadn't been waiting for me to find the right words. She'd been waiting for me to just—love her back. Big Guy opened the door just as our lips parted. I couldn't take my eyes off Oliver, or let her hand go. For the first time, I understood that the apocalypse was never going to be the end of the world as long as we stayed together.

"Come back to me," she whispered in my ear as she lay back down and let my hand go. She struggled to smile, and I knew I had to get moving. So I did. For her—I would find medicine. For Blake—I would find people who could help me kill my stepfather once and for all.

Big Guy and I took Loon Lake Road west toward the main highway. To pass the time, I listened to the crunch of dry gravel beneath the truck tires and Connor's panting. Big Guy drove fast and a little erratically. I wondered if he'd had any lessons before everything went to shit.

"Hey," Big Guy said, breaking the silence between us, "I know we're in a time crunch and all, but I need to do something in case my parents come back and wonder what happened to me."

"Okay," I said to him. We *were* in a time crunch, but there was also a good chance one of us—or both of us—

wasn't coming back. I completely understood why he'd want them to know what happened.

"I just want to leave a note for my dad. You probably think it's pretty stupid."

I shrugged. I wasn't arguing. Didn't need an explanation.

"I know we need to find medicine fast. I'm not trying to be a dick. I bet you think I'm such a dick."

"Of course I do." I tried to say this with a lightness to my voice as though it was funny, or maybe ironic. I smiled in a way that I had seen people smile when they joked. But Big Guy just kept this serious face and didn't say anything. No response other than his cheeks turning red. He didn't seem angry and I wondered why he kept talking.

"You know, if you and Oliver are gay—I just want you to know it's okay."

I tried to concentrate on the passing tree line as we turned onto the main highway. What Big Guy said made me think back to my books, to *Cue for Treason*, a story set in Shakespearean times, where a teen hid with a theater troupe to avoid being arrested. He meets a boy named Kit, who turns out to be a girl named Catherine. I tried to remember how he reacts when he finds out that Kit is a she and not a he, to learn if I should do the same. What I recalled was that he trusts her, before and after he finds out.

Even if our colony knew Oliver wasn't Oliver, she would always be in danger if someone stronger captured us. As long as the world thought she was a boy, she'd be safer in it. But more than that, what I knew was true was that my feelings for Oliver would not have changed if she had turned out to be a he.

"I don't know what's going on with him and me. Can we not talk about it?"

"Okay. How about we talk about that day I started pushing you around in back of the school?"

I let my burning cheeks answer for me. What did he think, that I didn't remember getting pounded as a bunch of kids cheered him on as if he were some prizefighter? As much as I tried not to dwell on it, I couldn't help but remember the times Big Guy had teased me at school. Especially the two times he had sought me out to beat me up. A part of me hated that he still believed he could take me.

"I did it because I had convinced myself that I was doing the school some big favor by punishing the weird kid. Or at least I think that's why I did it. Or maybe I did it because I wanted to prove to everyone that I was in charge of who was cool. I don't know."

"Why are you bringing all this up now?"

Silence returned between us, and I once again heard Connor's panting and the crunch of tires on the road.

"Because I'm sorry," Big Guy mumbled, and I saw his lower lip trembling. "I was really horrible to a lot of people who didn't deserve it. I was the worst to you. I didn't know how bad things were for you. I didn't know I was making things worse. I was this complete asshole, and here you are the one who saved me. And you did, you know. You saved me."

I had absolutely no idea what to do with what he was saying. Shake his hand? Punch each other's shoulders? I wasn't about to hug him as I would have Oliver. I had a suspicion this was coming out because of what had just happened to Blake.

"Don't worry about it," I finally said. "Let's just find out where these army brats are, and how much danger we're in."

Big Guy steeled himself. "Facebook status: 'Off to possibly die with the weird kid from school who has just become one of my best buds.'"

His last few words were said with a nod and a smile. I got the joke, but I didn't laugh.

The high school, a flat-roofed square building, all gray with windows that didn't open, was in a dip just on the south end of Clinton. Big Guy's home was just on the opposite side of the school from the highway, and so we cut through the field. When we drove past the football posts, I caught him glancing at them. I expected a fondness or sadness of a life he'd never get back. What I saw was a stern gaze—as if he was mad at them or something.

We entered his yard from the rear, but the back door was closed and locked. Big Guy fished around in his pockets. I realized he'd never given up his house keys. He was clinging to the last feeling of home he had. As he pushed a key in the lock, I took off for a quick run around the house. I checked windows and the front door—also I watched Connor's reactions for any sign of deaders. When I was satisfied we were safe, I went inside through the back door.

Big Guy was standing in the living room in front of a glass cabinet that held all his trophies. Had we come all this way just so he could see his stupid trophies? Other than the trophy case, the walls of the room were barren.

The paint was faded where pictures had once hung. The furniture was all upright and even crocheted doilies were centered on the end tables and backs of chairs. *Why would looters take personal photographs?* I took out my notebook to write down what I had just found, when Big Guy said, "They were here. They came back. They left. No note. Nothing. They left *me!*"

"What d'you mean?"

"I had a cough. My dad told me it was the Sickness. I told him I wasn't bit. He refused to believe me. I showed him—stripped right down while he screamed at me to put my clothes back on. My mom was crying."

Big Guy stopped talking. His breaths were so hard that he spat all over the glass trophy case. He clenched his hands by his side, and tensed his shoulders. "I was gonna leave them a note now, so when they came back they'd know I wasn't sick. But they came back already. They never even looked for me!"

"How do you know this?"

"Because they took the pictures. Who else would take the pictures?"

Connor scrambled behind me as Big Guy threw a chair at the trophy case. Glass scattered everywhere.

"I did everything he ever asked! Everything!" He fell to the ground. He wept into his hands. "Why didn't they leave a note? Why didn't they tell me where they went?"

For the first time, I understood that he'd also had it rough. He'd also had a father who had pushed him. He had a father just like all those in the books I'd read where the dad tried to live out his dreams of winning football trophies through their sons. That was why Big Guy was such a dick. The same reason I was such a dick to him.

Our dads.

"I'll wait outside. Take as long as you need," I said as I turned to leave.

He's a part of my colony, I said to myself and stopped before I reached the door. He was now a part of my family, and now we were each other's family. We all had lost everyone who mattered to us. Against everything that told me I was ridiculous, I approached Big Guy and wrapped my arms around him. As he cried, I stayed with him. To help him carry his sadness. When I shared this with him, he stopped being *Big Guy* and became *Tom*, my friend.

I drove the route toward Cache Creek from Clinton so Tom could process. We drove in silence. Tom—and that's what I would call him not only to his face but also in my thoughts—lay on the flatbed, alone, coddling one of his trophies. Connor sat on the bench with me. Ten minutes from Cache Creek, at the junction of the highway where it split southwest down 99, I saw them. I pushed hard on the brakes, and the truck screeched to a halt.

"What?" Tom asked through the back window.

I pointed ahead. The brats had two tanks parked sideways, blocking each road where the highway split. A couple of soldiers started walking toward us, shouting. No need to make out what they were saying—they wanted surrender.

"What now?" Tom asked.

"Stay in the truck, Tom. Stay with Connor. If things go south, turn the truck around and drive as fast as you can. When I'm able, I'll return with the medicine and soldiers."

"No way! I'm coming, too." Tom grabbed my shoulder through the window.

"If they let me in peacefully, yes you are. But if they shoot first, you need to help Kady protect Oliver."

I took my notebook out of my jacket pocket, but instead of writing in it, I threw it on the seat beside me. It was too important to take with me. It needed to be protected. Tom protested, asking inane questions. I ignored him and grabbed Connor by the muzzle. "Stay with Tom. Go home!"

Connor gave my face one lick, and I hoped he understood.

I leaped out of the truck and onto the road. Tom leaped out after me, but I dodged his hand grasping at me. I stuck to the center of the road as I approached the boys, my arms out and palms showing that I was not a threat. Connor scrambled behind me, and I cursed under my breath. He gave me a sharp glare, as if saying, "To the end. Together." I heard the truck behind me do a U-turn and then stop. Running, but not driving off. I hoped the army brats would be reasonable—up until the point when they readied their automatic weapons at me.

"So be it," I whispered to Connor. "I'm Bigwig. I'm Bigwig," I repeated this as a mantra, staying focused on the strong leadership character from *Watership Down*. The one who ultimately gives his leadership to the better-suited rabbit, just as I knew I would one day do for Oliver.

"HALT!" commanded one of the boys from on top of the tank.

I quickly counted ten guys and just as many girls dressed in camo. Half of them scrambled around to get behind me. Connor stopped beside me. I halted. Tom still hadn't driven away.

"Throw down your weapons!" The boy's words were followed by a gunshot that ricocheted off the ground in front of me. Connor jumped. I looked down at him and quietly said, "Run home!"

Connor scrambled to the side of the road, and as he fled, the army brats laughed. One of them pointed his gun at Connor. I drew a machete and threw it through the air at him. It hit the muzzle of the gun, causing him to miss when he fired.

"You said throw my weapons," I called back.

"Hold your fire!" the kid told his brats. He hopped from the tank and walked to me. "You're the one Timothy is looking for. Machetes. Dog. Yeah, you're the one."

His matter-of-factness was startling. Several of the larger boys grabbed me and pulled my weapons from me. I didn't struggle. As I heard Tom speed away, I knew this was exactly what I needed. This would get me into their base, and connected to any brats that wanted out.

CHAPTER NINETEEN

They took me to the once historic Hat Creek Ranch—what I would call Efrafa, the evil warren in *Watership Down*—with the two boys keeping their AK-47s pointed into my back. Now I knew where the army-clad deaders had come from. This was the perfect spot for the army to have taken over when the virus began. Situated east of the mountains, yet far enough in a valley that no one could station themselves in the hills to fight them. Windy enough that they had erected several wind turbines to keep electricity flowing—a ready-made campground with electricity hookups and a supply of horses to reserve fuel. I wondered where Timothy, my Woundwort, was and how he could have taken over this place.

We marched up to solid iron gates—the kind usually found around construction sites to keep looters out, with added barbed wire around the tops. Two kids on either side stood on watch holding AK-47s on either side. I wanted to write this in my notebook: four soldiers at the gates. As my captors talked to them and the gates opened, I spied metal towers that looked as if they were built from scaffolding. A metal ladder led up several flights of scaffolding to a fully exposed platform up top. A kid lay on her belly, one on each level, each armed with a rifle and binoculars.

One of the kids urged me forward with a push of his gun in my shoulder. The soldiers marched me slowly, as if they wanted me to see the force they had stationed on the one major highway through the north. I drew a mental map of the compound—the location of the bunkers, the mess hall, even the tent where I heard a movie playing. One of the only original structures was a white-washed barn with steel siding and a concrete base, behind what looked like the main lodge. Large fans replaced windows. *Must be a med center. Or a jail, perhaps.*

We passed one group of kids practicing how to shoot rifles, another where a girl was teaching wrestling, and a field where both football and dodge ball games were happening. I wondered if anyone was out in the fields growing food—surely, with electricity, the army brats would have kept the irrigation system active. Considering their numbers and how well organized they were, I began to doubt my chances of escape.

"We're taking you to a holding area first, where you'll be checked for bites," one of the boys behind me said as the two continued leading me at gunpoint into what appeared to be the main lodge—a colonial-style building with yellow wood paneling. Several kids with AK-47s resting against their chests paced back and forth along a white railing around the porch.

"Move it!" the guy behind me growled as he pushed the butt of his machine gun into my back. They hurried me inside, where they took me into a room and closed the door.

"Strip down. Put these on." One of the boys threw me an orange jumpsuit that looked like prison garb. I glared at him and he said, "Look, it doesn't please me, either. We gotta do it to stay safe. That's all."

I nodded in admiration at their dedication to one another. The virus was dangerous, and it would be an easy thing to sneak in an infected person who could turn in the night and destroy the camp. I remembered that was what Oliver had said started the original infection during New Year's Eve fireworks. One person was sick, and then two, then four, and then eight. After I had done as the soldier asked, the other soldier checked me over.

"What happened to your back?" the boy asked, as he scanned the scars.

I held the memories of what my stepfather had done in the shed at bay. When he finished, I put on the prison uniform instead of answering him.

They marched me back to the main hall and pointed up a flight of stairs. As I walked up them, the boy with the gun stayed positioned at the foot. I wondered what I was about to walk into and, again, remembered the book *Watership Down*. When Bigwig infiltrates Efrafa, he makes himself valuable by being able to fight. But the rabbits never had automatic weapons or tanks—and I had a feeling that I had no bargaining power. I'd landed in a hole that I wasn't going to be able to climb out of.

At the top of the stairs, I found a black-haired girl sitting at a long table and several boys, all armed, standing around it. On the table was a large satellite map of the area with several red circles drawn on it in marker. They'd circled Kady's home and the two farms with the dead people Oliver and I had stumbled onto.

"Your colony is here," Black-Haired Girl said, as she pointed to the map, right at my colony.

This is it, I thought, and prepared to die. I was just glad that Tom and Connor had gotten away. I hoped they had made it to Oliver, to help if there were an invasion.

"If you're going to kill me, then kill me quick. Don't bore me to death." I watched her eyes.

She looked down for a second before meeting my gaze head on. "Lucky for you, Timothy sees value in keeping you alive."

The way she emphasized *Timothy* made me assume she didn't agree. Black-Haired Girl smiled in the same way Kyle and Zeke had just before my stepfather took me to the shed for re-education. A shudder hit my body, transforming me back to that helpless boy—but only for as long as the shudder lasted.

"You remind me of the grown-ups," she said. "Cocky and so sure. Tell me, you think your friend won't break as easy? Tom, I think his name is?"

She threw my journal onto the table to show that he really had been captured. I lunged forward, but the click of a rifle behind me stopped me just shy of punching her out.

"I'm sure I could take you." Black-Haired Girl spat in my face. Then, to one of her lackeys, she said, "Take him to the dining area. Sit him at the guest table."

The soldier saluted and grabbed me by the arm. As I was pulled away, I managed to scoop up my journal.

At one time, Hat Creek Ranch was this tourist trap where city people could feel like a ranch hand for a weekend. Panhandling for gold in a nearby stream, fishing for trout in an artificially stocked lake, and trail riding on horseback.

The army brats took me to an amphitheater in what was once the entryway to the ranch. A parking lot filled with army vehicles was to our left, and a picnic area scattered with tables behind us. The tables were arranged in an oval around the amphitheater so all spectators had a glimpse of what was going on inside. I wondered what kind of entertainment they had planned. And suspected it had something to do with me.

I sat on a bottom bench in the amphitheater, with the dark-haired girl's "generals." Kids took seats along the rest of the benches, some too young to sit still, and some old enough to know better than to act restless. I couldn't help but wonder what had happened to the adults. Had they all died, or had there been a coup d'état? What had happened to the army that had taken this over as a base of operations?

The dark-haired girl was now in a box seat across from me, standing like a king overseeing a joust. Every person remained standing at attention, even long after she'd arrived. When she gave a nod, they all took their seats, clapping and hollering.

"We welcome a guest tonight, but before we break bread, we must attend to our business. It's important that our guest witness our justice."

Two guards bringing out a kid in chains with a burlap hood over his face quickly silenced the clapping and hollering. The kid staggered as he walked. He had open sores on his hands and arms. Blood stained his clothes, and dark purple bruises covered whatever skin showed. He shook—probably from both fear and cold.

The girl announced, "You are charged with high treason. You brought the infection into our colony, and you hid it from us. You endangered the entire group in an effort to save yourself. How do you plead?"

The boy started to cry. He dropped to his knees. He craned his neck toward jeers from a particular group of boys. They stared back, stone cold. From behind his hood, the boy faced the unwavering dark-haired girl.

"Please—please, Brianna. I was gonna tell you. I was gonna. I promise I was gonna . . ."

"Enough!" Brianna shouted. "You admit to your crimes, and now must suffer the consequences. We deal harshly with those who endanger our lives."

I had no doubt that last part was a jab at me. I wondered if Brianna expected me to attempt to save the boy, or to plead on his behalf for them to let him live. But who was he to me? Who but some stranger?

And then I felt as if Oliver's hand was in mine, squeezing it so tightly it hurt a little. She would have wanted me to do something about this. I couldn't help but want to make her happy.

"Take his life," Brianna said flatly.

A boy with a machete walked to the prisoner. Cheering rose from every table.

I had no weapons, but stones littered the ground at my feet. I grabbed one and threw it, directly hitting the guard in the hand. He cursed and dropped his machete. And I was over the table. Three guys were on me, but I knocked two away with a kick and punch. The third, I grabbed in an arm-bar, bringing him to the ground.

Then everything stopped as Brianna yelled, "ENOUGH!"

She smiled. The guy in chains was laughing. The guy who took the rock rubbed his fist. A wash of foolishness overtook me as I recognized the laughter. How was I the only one who hadn't seen this was all a test? I let the guy in the arm-bar free. When he stood, he shoved me.

They unchained the "prisoner." Before taking the empty seat next to Brianna, he removed his hood. The sores on his arms were make-up, which he wiped away with the burlap hood. The two guys I had knocked down also took seats, leaving me alone in the center.

"Stay where you are," the kid who played prisoner commanded me. "I knew I'd find you sooner or later. You remember me, yeah? Timothy. This group here is mine."

I stood in the center of the—and it had just hit me what it was—arena. Had they planned on torturing me publicly to show the people here they could make even me talk? At the end of the day, these kids wanted a show. The dried blood in the sod told me that Timothy hadn't been using fear to keep his subjects in line; he'd been using entertainment. I didn't even want to think about what he'd been doing to entertain his people—who he'd been killing. I considered saying something, but what was the point? I had no way out.

"Your stepfather has been a thorn in my side." As Timothy spoke, he walked toward me. "He says if I don't leave you alone, he'll kill me. Says if I don't leave you alone, he may not have to—because you'll kill me, yeah?"

He put his face right up to mine. When next he spoke, he spat. "Do you think you can kill me now?"

I considered head-butting him and breaking his nose. Instead I ignored him as he and everyone around me laughed.

"I could use you for bargaining peace from him. A gesture of good faith, yeah?" Timothy said this loudly to the crowd, and the kids went silent. Probably wondering what he was up to. Obviously, he was just saying this so that his next statement would make him sound stronger.

"I'll deliver you to him as a corpse. Throw your body on his doorstop so he never forgets who rules! The thing is, I just can't decide how I want to kill you."

Five of his goons brought out a stocky boy with bruised cheeks and one black eye. His hands tied behind his back. The crowd was going wild, banging cutlery on tables and jeering. It was Tom. They threw him to his knees. When they cut his hands free, he rubbed his wrists. He had bruises on his knuckles. I could tell by the glare that he gave Timothy that he still hadn't broken. He obviously didn't know that the army brats had figured out where our colony was and had probably sent a convoy to take Kady and Oliver out.

"In this corner," Timothy shouted, pointing at me as he stepped between Tom and me, "weighing in at 90 pounds soaking wet . . ." He gave me this look as though he hoped for me to say my name or to react to his childish insult. When I didn't say anything, he shouted, "Dead Man Walking!"

The kids laughed and banged cutlery on their tables. Then Timothy pointed at Tom and said, "In this corner weighing in at 200 pounds—"

"Get bent." Tom spat blood at him.

"Sack of Rubbish!" Timothy returned to his table, sat, and yelled, "You two will decide if I deliver Dead Man Walking to his father alive or as a corpse. But know this— one of you will be a corpse."

He paused and smiled at his audience before shouting, "DING! DING! DING!" as if he was the bell signaling us to battle. A rustle rippled through the kids, who were passing around what looked like candy bars.

"We're not fighting!" Tom shouted, as he walked up to me. He gave me a look that said *Right?*

But this wasn't some novel where a voice from above was going to make us a team and protect us from having to kill each other. *Deus ex machina* wasn't going to save us today. We had to put on a show, or Timothy was going to kill us both.

"Sorry, Tom," I said as I hopped back, crouched, and spun so I kicked him just behind his kneecaps. He went down, and the kids around us whistled and cheered.

Tom's eyes opened wide and he shook his head. I put up my fists, and his cheeks turned white. I knew what he was thinking—he was pleading that this wasn't happening. This wasn't the schoolyard where he could pummel me without consequences. He knew I could win—and that my victory in this would mean his death.

He was a football guy, so I readied myself for his tackle. Tom crouched low and hit me full-force with his shoulder harder than I'd expected. He landed on my chest, choking the wind from me. He hauled off to punch, but paused long enough that I could wrap my legs around his waist and butt my head into his skull. He shouted and brought his hands to his forehead. His next punch crossed my cheek. Before he could land a second one, I kicked my feet up around his neck. He flailed his fists at my stomach, but I grabbed his wrists and held him securely. As his face turned blue, I said to him, "I wish it hadn't come to this." And I actually meant it.

Children of Ruin

When Tom's body fell lifeless onto mine, I stood. Several of the army guys ran to drag Tom away, and Timothy applauded along with the other kids. Again, candy bars exchanged hands.

"Not even a competition, yeah?" Timothy again spoke to the other kids and not to me. "I can't believe how quickly you turned on—"

"Wait!" one of the brats dragging Tom away shouted. "This guy ain't dead."

Timothy turned red, even though he stayed composed. "What?"

"This guy ain't dead. I think he's just sleeping."

Timothy slammed his fist on the table. He growled at Brianna. "Take the quarterback and Dead Man Walking to the jail!"

Brianna stood and saluted, and then nodded at the brats nearest me. They came up behind me, and I let them tie my hands behind my back. My smile met Timothy's angry gaze head on, letting him know he hadn't broken me. He couldn't break me. And now that he'd seen what I could do, he'd think twice about trying to kill me himself.

"Make no mistake, you are going to die. Tomorrow we'll send you and the quarterback to the Pits, and you'll scream for mercy in front of everyone. We'll videotape it; send it to your stepfather to watch."

"The Pits?"

Timothy smiled. "Brianna, show our guest what fate awaits him tomorrow."

CHAPTER TWENTY

Brianna marched me across the compound with six heavily armed guards surrounding me. We headed toward a building that looked new—kind of like a big barn that had been erected quickly with steel paneling. A staircase led up to the only entrance I could see. When we were at the bottom of the stairwell, Brianna pointed to four of the guards and told them to leave. They glanced at each other. "NOW!" Brianna commanded.

They left, and I wondered what her end game was. Why leave herself more vulnerable with fewer guards in an area where I could probably escape without anyone seeing?

"Before we take you inside the Pits, I'm telling you this. Tonight, I'm taking you out of here with these boys and we're bringing you to your dad."

"What? Why . . .?" Even as I spoke, I had a feeling what was coming next.

Brianna grabbed my arms and shoved me toward the metal staircase. "In the land of the blind . . ."

As she said this, her minions followed with, "The One-Eyed Man is King!"

She started up the stairs and I followed her. I tried to piece together what was happening. I remembered my stepfather telling Timothy that one day his colony would hand itself over to him. It was actually happening. Brianna and these boys were converts. He must have promised them something that made siding with him more appealing than living here with Timothy. Whatever he had promised, she would never see it. Brianna betraying her colony made her a threat, not an ally, to my stepfather—knowing that she would switch for her own gain. And my stepfather did not take well to traitors. Even useful ones.

At the top of the staircase, Brianna looked away from me toward her colony busy at work. They'd all left the dinner, and were feeding horses, tending fields, or playing games of soccer or rugby. A wind I hadn't noticed till then carried the laughter and whispers that told me those kids were happy. With the right leadership, this colony could have been great.

She opened the door. We walked inside and along a mezzanine that surrounded the perimeter of the building. Every twenty feet an older teen in a lab coat sat on a chair scribbling on a clipboard. A guard was posted in each room on the corner of the building, and I smelled that rancid odor that could only be one thing—deaders. On the ground level deaders, maybe a hundred of them, walked aimlessly, snapping at the air. Women, men, and children.

"What the hell is this place?" I asked.

"Mostly our parents who caught the infection," Brianna said, "and many others we've captured."

The last part, she said with a red face. I wanted to believe her confession was embarrassment.

"Truth is, we have meds that can heal someone of a bite—but nothing that can cure someone of the infection itself. As long as you don't die, you don't turn. Timothy was bitten a month back, but no one but me knows."

"He told you this?" I asked, having a hard time believing her.

"No," she smiled, "He was bitten on purpose. We wanted to learn if he could become like the deaders, without being a deader."

"He thought he could become Spider-Man by being bit by a radioactive spider," I said.

"We kept Timothy alive by treating the bite. If he were to die now, he'd turn into one of the zombies."

That word. The one my colony didn't want to ever say out loud. When I heard it, even though it was exactly what they were, something just didn't feel real. Even though we'd been dealing with zombies for weeks, they still didn't seem possible. Calling them deaders made them feel less true.

"Did it work? Can he control them?" I asked.

Brianna watched where the guards stood. She kept an eye on them as they marched the mezzanine. One came close, and she grabbed me by the back of the neck and forced me to look down.

"See that? See it? That's our power!" she shouted into my ear. I didn't struggle, as her eyes darted from me to the guard telling me this was just for show. "He hasn't tested it for himself—yet. Timothy is turning more and more crazy, and now some of us want to escape," Brianna whispered to me. "Your stepfather has given us a place to go."

I opened my mouth to say something, but I noticed a girl sitting on the sod with her face in her palms. She was weeping, or at least appeared to be, as her back was doing that up, down, shudder-like movement that weeping people do. The deaders shuffled around her, sometimes sniffing her, but no more than they did each other. Every now and then the girl peered through her fingers at them, obviously aware of where she was.

"Oh my god, you put a kid down there who isn't infected."

Every fiber of my being wanted to fight my way down there and help that kid. But I'd be down there soon enough—the next day—and maybe, if they were still leaving the kid alone, I could figure out a way to save her. I found myself wishing Oliver were here, grabbing my hand and intertwining our fingers. Just imagining it made my heart stop racing. She gave me hope that everything would turn out okay.

"She's infected," Brianna told me. I looked again, expecting to see boils and rot on her flawless skin. She looked as scared as one would be who was in control of their every faculty. As if sensing my doubt, Brianna said, "She was our test subject. During early stages of the infection we treated the wound before gangrene or the flesh-eating bacteria killed her. We gave her some strong penicillin."

"And they won't eat her?"

"Are you getting it now? The infected don't eat, they spread. The virus only attacks those who could potentially spread it. Now you see Timothy's power. He could unleash all these infected and walk among them unharmed. He can lead them anywhere. Timothy—unstable, nothing-left-to-lose Timothy—could unleash all these on you. It's his weapon."

And my fate was to become a part of the weapon.

"You want to escape because you don't agree with him?"

She shoved me back toward the door and nodded for me to walk. Stepping out the door I squinted at the bright sunlight, and I paused before walking the metal staircase down. It wasn't easy with my hands tied behind my back, so I took each step slowly.

"My stepfather isn't going to help you."

Brianna nudged me with her hand. I nearly stumbled forward down the last seven steps. Once again we marched across the compound, passing kids as young as six or seven who, whether at work or play, all stopped to gander at me. I couldn't help but think about that little girl Oliver had tried to save. How much it had hurt her to have to end the girl's life, and what she would have done to be able to cure her. I wondered if we would have let the little girl stay had we known we could cure the wound and just keep her alive. I would have taken convincing, but Oliver would have taken the chance in a heartbeat.

I was led to a cabin with security bars drilled into all the windows and a deadbolt that locked from the outside. Two guards saluted Brianna. After she saluted them back, they opened the door and shoved me inside. Tom was sitting on a cot, his head in his hands. He was breathing hard. He didn't stand when he heard me. Not even after Brianna shut the door behind us.

"There's a small group of us leaving tonight." As Brianna told me this, she cut my hands loose. "We're taking you with us."

"Me?" I asked. "What makes you think I'll go without alerting everyone?"

Brianna laughed and stared at me directly in a way that would have made most people uncomfortable. The way I used to stare at my stepfather, until he got so upset that he brought me to the shed for re-education. Brianna replied, "Because you're stupid enough to believe you have a better chance of escaping on the run from us than from in here with Timothy."

I sat next to Tom. He looked over at me, his red-rimmed eyes and spit-covered lips betraying that he'd been crying.

"Just be ready," Brianna whispered, as she came nearer to us.

"My stepfather will kill you. If you wanted to get away, you could have joined us. I came here to see if any of you would join us."

"You're the losing team, you fool. Between Timothy and your stepdad, you are never going to survive. Why would anyone side with you?"

The door suddenly opened, and Brianna hauled off and punched me across the cheek. I collapsed to the cot just as a guard poked his head inside.

"Timothy wants a report," the guard told her.

Brianna walked out. After the door closed, I heard the click of the lock. I rubbed my cheek and got up and walked the few steps over to the other cot across the room. Nothing else was in there. No lamps, no toilet, nothing.

"Are we dead?" Tom asked just as I lay down.

Staring up at the ceiling, I considered his question. If Brianna got us to my stepfather, he'd kill us. If we stayed, Timothy would make us one of the deaders to use in his army. Brianna was our only chance to get out of Efrafa. She was right about me believing we stood a better chance escaping on the run.

"We're alive now, Tom. Don't give up."

He nodded, but I couldn't tell if he'd nodded because he forgave me, or if that was just how he coped. For now, I closed my eyes and decided to try and rest. When the escape plan happened, one of us needed to be ready. One of us needed to be aware enough to save both of us. To figure out when during the escape we'd need to *really* escape.

Muffled voices from outside the locked door woke me in the middle of the night. I listened hard to make out words, but it just sounded like noise. A shout and a bang against the door, as if a body had slammed into it, pushed me into peeling my blanket off me. I reached over to nudge Tom awake, but he was already wide eyed and sitting up.

"You okay?" I asked him.

"I'm ready," he told me. As a key clicked in the lock, he punched my shoulder, adding, "And we're okay. I get that you totally saved me."

When the door swung open, Brianna rushed in with two of her guards following close. One grabbed Tom's wrists; the other grabbed mine.

Tom gave me a look that asked, "Should we fight?" and I quickly shook my head. We allowed them to bind our wrists with nylon cable cuffs. We rushed outside and followed Brianna along the shadows of buildings toward the main gate. At the nearest building, Brianna checked her watch, and I saw her lips counting down. "Three, two, one . . . zero," she mouthed. As she spoke the last number, an explosion rocked the other side of the compound. Kids screamed and soldiers rushed with buckets of water.

Children of Ruin

"This is our chance!" Brianna said, and ran for the gate.

Tom and I followed as Brianna led us around the steel-sided building to the back, where we huddled beside a big door that looked like barn doors. Two of Brianna's army brats, each armed with an AK-47 and machete, walked behind Tom and me. One had a hockey bag like the one I had seen the girl at the auto shop with months before. For all I knew, any of them could have been the one who had shot Greg in the mechanic's shop or had killed the farmers. I had to remind myself that these kids were not innocent.

Brianna and I took the lead. I kept stumbling over roots that I couldn't see in the darkness and falling with my fists clenched out as a way to stop myself from face-planting. We couldn't turn on flashlights, as that would make us super easy to track. And we couldn't see any moonlight that far into the woods.

"Veer left here. There's a side road that parallels the highway," I told Brianna. I no longer concentrated on the guns behind me, as I just wanted to get as far away from Efrafa as possible. We were heading northeast enough that we would eventually come out at Loon Lake.

"We should stop to make sure no one is following," Brianna said. She held her hand up, signaling her boys to stop. They threw the bag down, and fell asses to the ground.

I objected. "We need to keep moving. What if we're being chased?"

Brianna glared at me, giving away that she might not be as honest about all this as she'd been pretending. Was Timothy crazy enough to think he could send Brianna as a spy into my stepfather's colony? As Brianna and I concentrated on our standoff, a group of deaders rushed at us from the bushes. One grabbed a brat and bit hard into his neck. The other army brat fired, and shadows in the woods fell to the ground. As bullets fired wildly, I met Tom in a huddle.

Brianna fired at the deaders, bringing them down with single shots right in their foreheads. I watched her posture as she fired, the way she held the gun, the way she listened to her surroundings after the bullet had fired. She was trained. Whether in cadets or by a military parent, or just a post-apocalyptic need to survive, she knew how to use that gun in her hands. If Tom and I ran, she'd have no trouble hitting us from a distance. Her actions also told me that she worried about Timothy knowing our location.

"Let me guess," I said. "Protocol is to send a handful of deaders after those who attempt escape. Outside the walls, the deaders will pick up the scent of those running—like bloodhounds—and when shots are fired Timothy knows where to look."

The kid who had been bitten was twitching on the ground. He gurgled, pleading for his life through the blood that pooled in his throat. Tears fell from his eyes. The last army grunt stared at Brianna. I wondered if this was the first time their own deaders had killed one of their own soldiers.

Brianna was on me fast. "This is your fault!" She got into my face and pushed me hard to the ground. I didn't struggle, and I couldn't fight back with my hands tied. "We would have heard them if you had just agreed to stop!"

I stood face-to-face with her again. "You wanted to stop to hear if any deaders had been sent our way. You are so over your head! Do you understand that you're heading off to be a lackey in my stepfather's colony, and you need me alive for your deal to stay solid?"

The kid on the ground still moaned. His eyes lolled into the back of his head. He was about to die. About to turn. But Brianna opened one of the hockey bags and grabbed a needle and vial. She filled the needle with what was in the vial. Then, slamming the needle into his leg, she pushed down the plunger. He stopped twitching.

"We're stopping." She growled through gritted teeth. To her brat she said, "Chris, look after Peter."

Chris sat and held a gun to Peter's head. "Just in case the medicine doesn't work," he told me. I could tell by his tone that he wasn't so keen on being the one to pull the trigger.

"We could rest at one of the abandoned roadside restaurants. Lots of them along the nearby road," I suggested. Brianna agreed, and Chris picked up Peter. I shook my head.

"We're not moving until you cut Tom and me loose. If Timothy is sending deaders after us, or if we wind up in a firefight, no way are we going down unable to protect ourselves."

"Right. And you try and run, escape, and I'm screwed. Don't think so."

"I'll make you a deal. I'll go with you willingly, no battle or fight, if you let Tom go free with one of the antibiotic kits in the morning. We have a friend who's dying, or might be dead, but her life is worth more than mine."

"Her?" Both Tom and Brianna asked, though Brianna spoke with a smirk.

"This is someone you love," Brianna said. "That's a deal I can trust."

Chris cut Tom and me loose, and we headed for the road. Tom sidled up next to me, but before he could say anything I shot him a look that told him to let it be for now. I needed him to do what I asked—to save Oliver. Even if it meant I ended up being delivered back to my stepfather.

When we emerged from the woods, and the moon gave us a little light, we found an old mom-and-pop kind of diner with a house attached to the back. I entered first, wishing I had Connor with me to sniff out any deaders who might be inside. The front door barely stayed on its hinges. As I opened it, I listened. Moonlight shone in through the front windows and across dusty tables and scattered broken jars, illuminating sugar, ketchup, and mustard spilled all over the floor. The place had been scavenged, meaning it could have been safe.

The others walked in after me as I made my way to sit on a stool at the front counter. Tom walked behind the counter, looked into the kitchen through a pass-through, and then rang a bell. "Order up!" he shouted. When no one laughed, he leaned on the counter opposite me. He gave me a long look that told me he had gone behind the counter on purpose. Here, we could shift the power back to us.

Brianna and Chris, carrying Peter, stumbled into the dining area and glanced out the window. They put Peter on the floor after kicking away a few empty plastic ketchup bottles. The sun had begun to rise, changing the cobalt blue light to a dull shade of amber.

"Don't do anything," I whispered to Tom.

Brianna snapped me a hard glare. I wondered if she had heard me. She patted her gun, still holstered at her side.

The rest happened so quickly it was a blur of reactions. Tom threw the meat cleaver that he'd found behind the counter. He missed Brianna, whom I assumed he'd chucked it at, and the stray weapon wound up slamming into the floor.

Brianna drew her gun, but I instinctively slammed into her and knocked her to the ground. As she lost balance, she fired one shot. Chris moved in, but the cleaver had landed on Peter and had killed him. That turned him— treated with medicine or not. Chris fired at the now-deader, leaving Brianna struggling against my grip. I wrestled Brianna and brought her gun hand up on Chris. Brianna fired before she knew what she was doing.

"Give me your weapon!" I commanded her, as Chris fell to the ground.

"Let me help him!" Brianna shouted, struggling to get free. I pulled her down to the ground and held her in an arm-bar.

Finally she stopped struggling, and I took away her gun. I set her free, and she fished another needle from the hockey bag. Brianna rushed to Chris, who was shot in the arm, and pushed the needle into his leg. "This should keep you alive until we get to Evergreen Fishing Resort. Someone there should know how to take a bullet out of your shoulder."

"Tom, that was a huge chance!" I said.

"Facebook status: 'Kind of like the weird kid who runs my colony. Not ready to let him die.'"

"We're leaving right now," I told them. To Brianna I said, "We'll still take you to my stepfather's colony, but we're not going the whole way with you. You can tell him you failed."

Tom took a knife off Brianna and a gun and Bowie knife off Chris. He tied our prisoners' wrists with nylon cuffs he found in the bag, and I gathered our weapons. I also found my notebook and immediately set to writing down everything that had happened.

After a few hours had passed, no one—human or deader—had been by the restaurant. Tom and I, now fully armed and ready, began the march back into the woods with our prisoners. Tom carried the hockey bag of medicine, the bag that would save Oliver if she was still alive, over his shoulder. I watched everywhere, around the hills and as far down the road as I could. Dark clouds were moving in. The air had turned cold and crisp. The nearer we got to the lake, the thicker the fog that rolled in. No doubt Timothy was now close on our heels, having heard the gunfire from the night before. He needed to bring us back to save face, else my stepfather's psychological warfare would, indeed, win him Timothy's colony.

Two giant egos fighting for supremacy. Two giant egos I could use to destroy each other.

CHAPTER TWENTY-ONE

Tom and I took Brianna and Chris to the gibbets where Timothy, or my stepfather, could find them. The remains of men and women rotted inside the cages, some with bullet holes to the brains and others fully intact, indicating those people hadn't had the sickness and had died of starvation and exposure. Every cage had pin-tumblers, locks with grooved keys that, when pushed downward, aligned all the cylinders inside the lock. I didn't have a key, but my stepfather had taught me how to pick locks. I was pretty good with a pin. I pried a needle from the med kit into one of the locks. It took me a few tries, but eventually it clicked open.

"Now what, remove the dead body and throw in our live ones?" Tom asked.

"Nope."

With my machete, I sliced the cable tying our prisoners' hands together. Then I grabbed Brianna by the hair. She struggled. I pushed her face first into the gibbet, grabbed her feet, and hoisted her body the rest of the way inside. She screamed and I worked fast. I slammed the door and closed the lock. I did the same with Chris.

"You need to get back to Oliver and Kady," I told

Tom. I pointed at the bag of medicine.

"No. I'm not leaving you behind."

"We need to get this med pack home. I need to make sure my stepfather finds these two."

"And then what?" Brianna spat out. "Then I get to watch him kill you?"

I opened the hockey bag and fished out a flare gun. I threw the bag to Tom. "When Timothy realizes we got this far, he'll think my stepfather outdid him. He's all about winning, and he's so crazed for power he doesn't care who he hurts. His pride won't let him lose. He'll have to strike."

The loaded flare gun was ready. I fired. A long streak of red flame lit up the sky, drowning out the sun, showing everyone where to find us.

"Now my stepfather knows where to find me. So does Timothy."

"If you're not back by noon, I'm coming to get you," Tom said.

A part of me wanted to tell Tom that he was wrong. That if I wasn't back by noon, it was because I was dead. The right thing to say was that he had to forget about helping me. But as Tom and I nodded at each other, I knew he needed to feel as though he'd rescue me if necessary. And he needed me to believe he'd do it. I hoped this wouldn't be the last time we spoke as he turned and walked into the woods.

My mind turned to what I needed to do. My heart raced. I didn't want to do this alone. I wished I had Connor with me. Chances were he was dead. Doubtful he would have made it home after his escape from Efrafa. But now, it was just me. Waiting for my stepfather, and for Timothy. Waiting to start the war that would end the struggle over this territory.

I sat in the woods where I was hidden but could still see whatever happened. I was doing what my stepfather was so good at—playing mind games to pinpoint weaknesses. This one was a big gamble for me, but if these two forces canceled each other out, it was worth taking. If I could get my stepfather to fight the army brats, if I could get the two sides to kill each other, I might never have to deal with either of them again.

Rustling sounded from the bushes in the direction of my stepfather's colony. First, a couple of men stepped out, each one brandishing a rifle. Then two more. Lastly my stepfather. Seeing him in person, that scarred face missing one eye, boiled my blood. Memories of my mother and sister consumed me. I pushed down the need to rush him, to hack down on him with my machetes. To spit in his face as I reminded him that I had triumphed over his two sons.

He walked up to the gibbet with Brianna. He looked at her hard with his one eye, and I saw that his skin was dried and cracked.

"What do we have here?" he whispered, in that voice that would have gotten me hit if I had answered him. It was a type of voice where he asked questions he did not want to be answered. "Did you not understand our deal?"

Brianna grasped the bars but didn't say anything. She could have easily given me away, told my stepfather I had taken to the bushes. Her fear was so strong it almost radiated from the gibbet. After all her yelling and screaming, her wide eyes showed that her fear had rendered her speechless.

My stepfather began one of his rants. "You are not

what you seem! You are a trickster. Something that makes me look right, when I should be looking left." He grabbed the bars over Brianna's fingers. She winced and struggled to pull free. "Our deal was not to deliver *you*. It was to deliver *my stepson*. Who then delivered you to me, unless it was my stepson?"

Brianna nodded but still did not speak. When I clicked the gibbet shut, I killed her. Maybe not instantly, but by delivering her to my enemy. And now I regretted it. Regretted that I knew her death would not be quick, nor would it be justice. For that moment when I sentenced her I had forgotten that she was a person. When she had acted like a monster, like an unfeeling beast, this had been an easy decision. But not now. Now, she seemed like a scared teenage girl who was wishing her parents would come and save her. I now wished that I could save her.

"You stare at my eye. Or where you see no eye." My stepfather pressed his scarred face against the bars. "Do you see an eye?"

Brianna shook her head. My stepfather laughed. "That is because you are blind." He finally let her go, and she tucked her hands into her jacket. My stepfather continued his rant. "You are all blind. Only I can see. We live in the land of the blind . . ."

"Where the One-Eyed Man is King," his soldiers chanted in unison. Chills trickled down my spine.

"You!" He pointed at her. "You have trespassed onto king's land without the proper tribute. Let me see your hands."

Brianna shook her head and kept her hands tucked into her jacket. She glanced over at me in the bushes.

"No one is here to help you," my stepfather said. "No

one but me. Show me your hands, and I will set you free."

"You'll . . .let . . .me . . .go?" she whimpered. I wondered just what my stepfather had done to their colony to make her this afraid of him.

"You have my word."

Brianna slowly took her hands from her jacket and squeezed them through the bars up to her shaking wrists. Palms up.

"Can I go now?" she asked.

In a blur, my stepfather took a machete from inside his coat and brought it down on her wrists. Someone screamed, but it wasn't Brianna. Timothy had found his way to us, and had now opened fire. My stepfather took cover behind his men and fled into the woods with them. They fired back. Bullets flew everywhere. I took off, too, now knowing my two enemies would fight it out. Hopefully killing each other. Hopefully ending it. Hopefully justifying this awful thing I had just done.

I ran along the deer trail near the trapper's cabin so I wouldn't make noise crashing through the brush. The sound of gunfire echoed in the woods behind me. I darted down the path until I reached our home.

"It's Ethan!" Tom yelled from the roost when I was in the middle of the clearing.

Kady burst from the door, and Connor was so fast behind her that he almost tripped both himself and Kady. I couldn't believe he was here, that he'd made it back. I fell to my knees, and he leaped on me and licked my face. I hugged him hard. My eyes might have even teared up I was so happy. But it was a happiness short lived, as I was almost too afraid to ask . . .

"Is Oliver—"

"Alive and stable, thanks to that medicine!"

Gunfire cracked. Closer. And it sounded less and less like a fight. First the bang of rifles, followed by the *rat-a-tat* of machine guns. Soon, just rifle fire. My stepfather was driving away the army brats. I would have to return to Evergreen Resort to see if my plan to save us had worked—but even if it had, at what cost? What kind of war had I started?

Kady, Conner, and I rushed through the front door. I scrambled to the roost. "Protect Oliver!" I shouted, and Kady and Connor rushed to Oliver's room. Tom aimed his riflescope on the surrounding woods, and I picked up a pair of binoculars. I listened. For gunfire the way one would listen for thunder. The longer the pause between bursts, the more likely the fight was done. I kept my eyes on the woods, but no one else was coming. I slowly dropped the binoculars, and then fell to my rump.

"Facebook status," Tom whispered. "'I miss when it was just deaders.' What now?"

His voice shook, and I knew he was scared. He should be. We had just declared war on the two biggest neighboring colonies. If my stepfather had survived, he wouldn't play mere games to test me after this. And when the army brats returned, they'd return to conquer. As for a plan, I had none, except . . .

"Survive the day," I said.

I left Tom on watch and walked to Oliver's room. Kady was beside her, and when she saw me, she met me at the doorway. Connor sat by Oliver's bedside, ears perked, the perfect watchdog.

"She's weak," Kady whispered, "and who knows if she's out of the woods yet. I'm no doctor. I guessed at how to give her the medicine."

"She?" I asked Kady.

"I had to change her dressing to smear the antibiotic on it. Yeah, I know."

I nodded, and as Kady left the room, I sat beside Connor at Oliver's side. Her eyes were closed, red-rimmed, and her breaths were raspy. She was so pale. Immediately the sight of her washed away any guilt I might have felt over the deaths I'd caused that day. *They did this to you.* The army brats. My stepfather. Why couldn't they have just left us alone to live in peace?

Oliver reached out and brushed my hand with her fingers. I took her hand and squeezed it. She opened her eyes, and I tried to tell her to just sleep. But when I opened my mouth, any words I tried to say caught in my throat.

"I knew you'd make it back," she said and smiled.

"I wasn't going to leave you . . ."

"Or your dog." She laughed and coughed at the same time. "When Connor returned, I knew you'd be back. You love that animal."

I recognized this as a joke, a way of bridging all those things we wanted to say to each other but almost never had the chance to. I closed my eyes tight as this pressure built in my head, but all I could see when I did so was her body lying on the ground with a bullet hole in the shoulder. I opened my eyes when her fingers left my hand and softly brushed my cheek.

"I love you," I told her. The words were painful for me to say. I'd never heard them said to me, or to anyone actually, let alone ever had a reason to say them to someone. I knew I loved my mom and my sister, but to tell them was to show weakness. To show weakness meant a lesson in the shed. But there I was, with Oliver—and I knew that I loved her.

Oliver nodded and smiled. Closed her eyes. But as she drifted back to sleep she said back, "I know." And again she chuckled as if from a joke that I just didn't get. The funny thing for me was that I didn't need to hear her say it back for me to know that she loved me, too. Somehow she'd told me she loved me long before this moment. Without the words. Simply by the way she always treated me. By the way she trusted me. From the first moment on that credit union roof until now.

When I returned to the roost, Kady was scanning the woods with the riflescope while Tom lay fast asleep tucked into a sleeping bag. He'd most likely passed out from exhaustion—both physically and emotionally. I didn't envy him his dreams. Standing watch all day was something we'd been doing for months, but we weren't going to last long now that we were sure someone out there wanted us dead. I watched for any movement in the woods.

I knew my stepfather well enough to not expect an attack that day. He'd want a fight, one that would bring him real victory. One that might even make a name for him in this new world. I wondered what kind of reputation *I* had in this new world. Did my stepfather talk about me? To him, I would always be the boy who killed his sons. The cub he should have killed when he took over my mother's pride.

Now, once again, I had hit him hard where and when

he did not expect to be hit. Maybe he respected me more because of it. The next night would be a big night—even if the war did not come to us, we would have to go to it. We could hope to hide no more.

"Hey," Kady whispered, "I think it's going to rain. Clouds have covered all the stars."

"We need to run." My voice was flat, as I didn't want Kady to know that I feared my stepfather. So long as she thought I wasn't afraid, she'd have the strength to keep going forward.

"How far can we run before meeting a man just like your stepfather? When do we stop running?" she asked.

For the first time, I saw that Kady was truly ready to use the rifle. Somewhere along the way, we all had changed. All of us, including Kady. It could have been from the fight lessons that Oliver had given her, but I believed her asking for fight lessons in the first place had started her change.

"I have lived more in these past weeks than I did my whole life," I told Kady. "Thanks to all of you."

"You're not done yet," she said sternly. "We're not done yet. I'm ready to fight back, but we need you to get some rest so we can figure out a plan of action."

I knew where we needed to hide. My sanctuary, my fortress of solitude. "There's a trapper's cabin deep in the woods. Oliver knows where it is. We need to take our supplies, bare minimum, and get to the cabin. My stepfather doesn't know about it—and maybe, just maybe, we can sit out the war and let the army brats and the One-Eyed King kill themselves."

Kady scrunched up her forehead and let out a long sigh. She had to know I was right, but what I was hoping was that she didn't realize my secondary plan. No way I was letting my stepfather off easy. A bullet to the head? That wasn't what he deserved after killing my mother and my sister. He deserved to suffer vengeance at the hands of the boy he believed too weak to bring into the apocalypse.

"We won't stop you," Kady said quietly. "At least I won't."

A memory of her first scream, the one that sent me running across the field to her rescue, filled my mind. The girl in front of me now was not that same kid, that frightened child needing someone to protect her. Now she stood tall, rifle in hand, ready to fight. The hard look in her gaze told me that she knew my plan. She knew I was going after my stepfather before someone else got to him first.

"Ethan?"

"Yes?"

"Say goodbye to Oliver. She deserves that much. And Ethan?"

"Yes?"

"I'll take care of her. I'll protect her."

Kady's words were how I knew she didn't expect to see me come back. She didn't expect me to win.

CHAPTER TWENTY-TWO

I headed for the door, stopping outside Oliver's room. I stared at the closed door, wondering if I should go inside. She'd know I left when Kady came to fetch her, and she'd be hurt if I didn't say some sort of goodbye. But if I did that, if I said goodbye, would she talk me out of going?

"You're not going alone," Tom said, startling me back to the moment.

"You need to stay and protect them," I answered, without turning to face him. "Oliver is still sick and weak from—"

"Kady is able to protect herself—"

"*You can't come.*"

As those words left my lips, Connor sauntered up beside me. I patted his head, maybe to show Tom that I wasn't going alone. I turned to Tom and could tell by the look on his face that he knew I was saying goodbye. That, just as Kady believed, I really didn't expect to win.

"I'm not afraid to die," he said in a shaky voice.

"Tom, I'm not ready to watch you die. Say goodbye to Oliver for me."

Before he could speak again, I rushed out the door into the darkness with Connor. Machine guns and rifles still battled it out, so I fled into the woods, hidden from view. A fog rolled in along the ground, limiting my visibility so I couldn't see patrols or soldiers or deaders. The humidity and cold soaked into my black armor, beading into my hair, and as I wiped it away, I also wiped away mosquitoes biting my skin.

I couldn't think about any of that now as Connor and I pushed our way through dense brush. *Stay silent. Find the way so they won't expect me.* Throughout the woods, I stumbled on dead army brats strung up in trees. Arms and legs spread out. A rope leading from each limb to a tree.

As I neared the farm, I heard the sound of cows and chickens. The brush thinned the closer I got to it, and soon I could peer into the colony. I could clearly see the farmhouse tucked into the far side of the clearing, nestled near the lake. And the fences separating cows from bulls, and the coop filled with chickens.

The two men who'd almost killed Kady were wandering the yard, no doubt looking for army brats. They were carrying shotguns and watching their surroundings nervously. If they weren't ready for possible retaliation, they were at least fearful of it. I reached into my pack and took out the night vision goggles, peering into them to see if I could spot a lookout.

The top of their house didn't have a roost and the attic window appeared shut. I didn't see anything else that looked like a roost until I peered into the trees. I saw someone sitting in a bow-hunting platform, which was little more than a chair fastened fairly high up a tree. He was armed with a bow, scanning the area with binoculars. He didn't seem alerted, so he couldn't have spotted me. I wondered how many other lookouts I couldn't see.

As I nestled into the dirt with Connor beside me, I heard someone shouting. A man. At first I couldn't make out whom. Then the man brought a group with him, armed with rifles, running in my direction. When they were closer, I heard, "There! See him? He's there!"

My heart raced. *I'm caught.* My hands went to the hilts of my machetes. But the men veered far to the left of me. I knew it wasn't me they'd seen. It was Tom, deep in the brush, who stood with his arms up. He had followed me, making me wonder how I hadn't spotted him. Thanks to the fog, the men didn't see me. More men and women emerged from the house, rifles drawn and pointed, and I knew Tom was in trouble. If I helped him, both of us would get killed. "Run!" I whispered, wishing I could shout it to him.

"Step out of the bushes!" one man shouted.

Tom turned to bolt, but he had waited too long. Multiple shots rang out. My only hope was they were loud enough to reach my colony so that Tom's needless death wasn't meaningless, and Kady and Oliver would know to get to the trapper's cabin.

Tom's body fell to the ground with a thud. "Get rid of this," a woman told two others. Without questioning the order, they dragged Tom toward the back of the house.

Tom had made this decision himself, acting like the friend we had both sworn we'd never become. A friend who had paid the ultimate price. I filled with anger. With rage. He didn't deserve such an end. It was all I could do to stop myself from rushing out and taking down as many of them as I could right then and there. But I didn't. Even though the game had changed. Before, to take my stepfather's seat at his king's table, I had killed my stepsiblings. Tonight, I was poised to take the head seat at the table—and to do that I had to kill my stepfather.

For my mom. For my sister. For Tom. I waited. Patiently.

As the darkness got longer, my head started to whirl. Exhaustion was hitting me. A previous sleepless night, sitting all day beneath the hot sun, sweat soaking me beneath my armor. Now, fatigue and chills fell on me all at once. My eyes were forcing themselves shut, and the cooling air forced me to shiver so hard I thought it could be heard a colony away.

This was not the time to deal; I couldn't be weak. I forced myself to forget my body as the time approached to complete my task. The moment where everything would change completely—where *I* would have to change completely. Where I'd turn from protector to executioner. When the world would truly end.

The lookout I'd spotted started smoking, and now two more cigarettes were glowing. One man was on the opposite side of the entry road; the other faced the back of the house. A woman sat in a tree just to my left. The house had no lights, though that might have been more to preserve candles than the attic not being a lookout. My stepfather, though smart and prepared, was predictable to someone like me. Someone who'd listened to all the lessons he gave my stepsiblings. Even without seeing anyone, I knew where the sentries were posted.

Next, I had to be fast and methodical. Any hesitation

might cost me my life. I couldn't leave any of them alive, or I'd be watching over my shoulder for retaliation all my life. My goal was simple: protect Oliver, Kady, and myself so we could build again.

I searched my pack for the slingshot and took out three metal balls. It was dark, so the lookouts' cigarettes were my targets. All I saw of the lookouts were the glowing tips as they rested low, and then rose and ignited brightly. I had to shoot, when the tips were at their brightest.

First I would shoot the woman above me. Had it not been for her cigarette, she might have gone unnoticed. But, as the package says, smoking kills. I leaned onto my side carefully so I wouldn't make any noise. I pulled back the elastic and aimed the ball at the red light. When her cigarette glowed bright red, I released the ball.

No scream. No gasp. No whimper. Just a red-tipped glow falling to the ground as she let go of the cigarette. Crawling beneath the lookout, I peered through my binoculars at the other posts. Their red tips glowed steadily, and I assumed they hadn't been alerted. The cigarette the woman had dropped started to smoke in the dry brush. I reached over with my boot to tap it out. Last thing I needed was a forest fire. For a moment I thought about Mowgli getting fire to fight Shere Khan.

The other two were closer to each other than this woman was. I decided to go for the one watching the house before the one watching the lake. I needed to cross the field—and somehow do so unnoticed. I rose into a squat and moved slowly out of the brush. Connor followed. There were no lights in the yard nor could I hear any generators running. No electricity meant they were dependent on candlelight. Clouds that covered the moon stole away all natural light, though I still hoped none of these lookouts were accurate shots.

I sidled against the silent chicken coop, pressing myself against the wooden frame. One of the nearby lookouts turned on a high-beamed flashlight, passing it over the yard. If I moved he'd spot me and force me to change my plan. The light suddenly went off, and he flashed a red beam three times. I counted a three-second pause, and he did it again. The lookout tower by the lake did the same. Now I was in trouble. They were waiting for the woman I had just killed to flash hers. I could have tried to make it to the woman's post. Climb the tree. Flash her beam. Which would have been stupid. They'd have been on me before I made it to her body.

I had no other choice than to go in fast and hard. "Stay!" I told Connor, as I didn't want him out in the open until I knew it was safe. I grabbed the hilt of my two machetes and drew them out. I heard that Hollywood sound of *shhhhfft* as the metal rubbed against the leather sheath. My heart pumped faster. My eyes looked everywhere. I didn't know who to hit first.

A gun fired. I spun to face the sound, just in time to see a shadow running from the road to the bushes. Was it the army brats? I hoped Kady hadn't come looking for Tom. The lookout nearest me started to fire toward the road. A siren blasted loudly throughout the compound as all the lookouts started firing at the road. A *rat-a-tat* of machine gun fire from behind me, and the siren fell quiet. More army brats.

Five armed women rushed from the house and scattered throughout the area. One dashed behind a truck, another scrambled for the lookout tower, a third ran toward the lookout I had killed. The other two moved into the yard. The last one headed toward me. I crouched and waited. I hoped she was focused on the soldier at the road. She rounded the corner, and without hesitation I swiped with my machete. It was silent. It was efficient.

It was the first kill I had to see full on. I froze. It was indescribable as to what happened to me at that moment. I wished I could take back those last few seconds of my life. *This is why you will die*, my stepfather's voice said in my head. It was just enough to snap me from my trance, as a rifle bullet grazed my cheek. I fell against the coop again and pressed my body flush against the wood. Heavy steps came toward me, and then another rifle blasted. I heard no more steps.

The person on the road could deal with those in the compound. I needed to get into that farmhouse where candlelight flickered through the windows. If any were oil lamps I may be able to use them to burn the home to the ground. I held my blades with my arms straight, and touched the tips to the sod. My breathing steadied. My heart calmed. I started toward the house but stopped when a figure emerged.

"In the land of the blind . . . the One-Eyed Man is King!" the figure spat.

CHAPTER TWENTY-THREE

"You killed my boys." His words were calm, spoken through a clenched jaw. Dripping with his hatred for me. We stood only a few strides apart, both of us soaked by the rain that suddenly pelted from the sky. When I had dashed into the shelter, when I had chosen to save myself rather than stay and fight for my mother and my sister, I had hidden from this moment. A few months before, I'd been just a boy. Now, I was ready to be a monster.

"I was more worthy than them." I had to scream this over the storm that raged around us. Cobalt clouds hid the stars, and the wind whipped raindrops across my cheeks and into my eyes. To show him I wasn't going to run again, I held out my machetes so he'd see them clearly. "I don't care if you find me worthy! I don't care anymore!"

All that time I had spent at the dinner table, wishing I could be where his sons sat, seemed pointless now. I was never going to be worthy. I was not of his blood. Even though I couldn't hear him above the rain, I knew by his grin that he was laughing at me. That he had no fear in his blood from this battle. That he was confident he knew the outcome. That his one prophetic eye had told him that he would reign as king, with my head on a stick to warn others who might oppose him. Slowly and with purpose, he drew a machete of his own. He staggered his feet and motioned with his hand for me to come at him.

I understood him. As much as he wanted me to see he had no fright, I knew he was the angry one. The one who had dreamed of this fight. The one who had spent all his time sending me messages to psychologically break me. Did his colony know why he wanted me dead so badly? What lies had he told them to keep them under his control?

He rushed me. Machetes clashed and rainwater sprayed. A small burst of sparks flew as metal scraped against metal. He swung his body and knocked me onto the ground, but I managed to pivot just enough to avoid him. I sliced at the back of his legs, but my stepfather was too fast. The bunt of his machete crossed my face, and suddenly I smelled my own vomit. The blows came quick, and with each I found it harder and harder to stand. The world spun, and just as I started to collapse, his strong hands pulled me back up.

"What did you think? You'd come here, fight me, and avenge your pathetic colony?"

Yes. That was exactly what I'd thought.

"I've been watching since the day you crawled out of that hole. I've watched every mistake. Every moment that led you here to your demise."

He pointed the tip of his machete on my chest. I managed to open my eyes enough to see his madness. I reflected on my mom and sister. Blake and Tom. Even Kady and Connor. Mostly, I reflected on Oliver, and how I wished I could have had one more time to say goodbye. To say thank you. The One-Eyed King was going to kill me, and I could do nothing about it.

"You destroyed everything I loved." His voice was wet

with sadness, but for only as long as it took to spit out the words, "You killed my sons!"

The tip cut into my skin, and I closed my eyes for the end.

But there was no end, no darkness. He wrenched to the side and tossed me to the ground. Growling filled the bits of silence between raindrops as my eyes focused on Connor, who was clenching his jaw on my stepfather's wrist. My stepfather screamed so loudly that I imagined Conner ripping the flesh right to the bone. This was my one chance to flee. My one chance to live.

"Connor! Come!" I called, and scrambled to my feet. My feet slipped in the wet grass as I scurried back to the woods. My body bounced on the ground and off the trees, but I made my way in the dark as best I could.

Gunshots fired more rapidly. The fight was heating up. Maybe the army brats would win, and I'd only have *them* to worry about. As I ran wildly through the trees, their branches scraping against my skin, I heard a yelp that burned into my soul. More painful was the silence that immediately followed—a silence that knocked me to the ground.

"Connor," I whispered, knowing he hadn't followed me. I gripped my hair tightly in my fists and howled, knowing this was how my stepfather had felt when his sons didn't return from hunting me. I now had the same knot of revenge in my heart to see *him* dead. I forced myself to stand and stumble forward.

At last I saw the lodge. Perhaps because of the darkness, I had expected to find Connor there. Exhaustion hit me and my knees buckled. It was as if the ground were falling toward me as I collapsed onto the dirt. I managed to catch myself from falling past my knees, but I'd come as close to the lodge as I could. The machetes on my back were heavy, as if they were pushing me to the ground. My arms shook from holding myself up, and now I was ready to give up.

Tears and rain on my cheeks confused me into thinking Connor had run to my side. It was his tongue licking my face, his nose nudging me in the ribs, him saying, "Thank you for all you did for me."

My eyes shut, and my cheek sank into the mud. "Good-bye, Connor," I muttered. "Good-bye, my friend."

The smell of canned stew reached my nose just before I heard the sound of it bubbling on a hotplate. At first when I opened my eyes, I expected to see my mom in her pink floral nightgown making breakfast for her hungry family. This feeling took me back to before the accident that had changed my stepfather. When my mom was pregnant with my new half sister, and my stepsiblings were trying to figure out how to be my friend.

I saw my mom's smile, heard my stepsiblings' laughs, and listened as my stepfather spoke of future vacations and making memories together. We were happy. But as the memory began to turn into a haze, my mom's eyes became bruised, my stepsiblings stood over me glaring, and I watched as my toddler half sister followed my stepfather into her room, and my stepfather closed the door behind them.

I was brought back to the present with memories of the deaders, of my zombified sister, and of Connor's sacrifice. Of Blake murdered, Kady turned, and Tom executed. And the faces of all the people I'd had to kill. I wasn't in a home with a family, once loving, who'd turned dysfunctional. I was on a cot in the hunting lodge. Gripping the sides of the bed to push myself up. Forcing away sleep. My eyes focused as Kady cooked breakfast.

"I was sure everyone was dead," she said, without turning to face me. The crackle in her voice told me she'd been crying. I recognized it from the times I had heard my mother cry. "Tom ran off after you. I watched him from the roof. I couldn't stop him—"

"He's dead," I interrupted her, though I knew that she knew.

Her knees buckled for a second before she regained her composure. "I know you tried to save him." Kady repeated this over and over again. Quieter each time she uttered the words. How could I tell her that I hadn't? I couldn't tell her.

I swung my legs over the cot. When my bare feet touched the floor, I realized I was in my underwear and T-shirt. Oliver was on another bed against the opposite wall opposite me. She was sleeping, her chest rising and lowering steadily. Color was back in her cheeks. I was thankful in a way that I had never imagined I could be thankful.

"I cleaned you up while you were asleep," Kady said, scooping some stew into a bowl. "I didn't know what else to do."

I watched her walk to my cot carrying only one plate of food. Chances were she wasn't going to eat because she couldn't. Not because she had already. It was strange for me to get the first plate of food. The lion's share.

"I'm glad you got away," I said, taking the food and

shoveling it into my mouth. My hands were shaking, making it difficult to eat.

"They came. So many. But we fled just in time. Oliver was able to stay awake long enough to show me the way here." Tears rolled down her cheeks, and she buried her face in her palms. "I think she's okay."

I had nothing left to save. My colony decimated, our home overtaken. For now, the poacher's cabin would keep us safe. But for as long as my stepfather knew I was alive, he'd be hunting me. It still rained, but more calmly now. It didn't seem much different than the gunfire on our tin roof, except that when the rain hit, no holes burst through.

We needed a plan. I needed to think. I took out my soaked notebook and saw that the ink had run through the pages. My body rocked back and forth, and a pressure built in my head. This was all wrong! In all the comics I'd read, the hero always won. The hero always saved his family and his friends. The hero didn't lose as I had just lost.

"It's okay," Oliver whispered from her cot. I took a blanket and wrapped it around my trembling shoulders. As I kneeled beside Oliver, she turned her head toward me, her eyes fluttering open. Her chapped lips parted into a smile. I stayed beside her, and she reached out for my hand. Our fingers entwined. My heart beat fast and hard. She sat up and rested her head on my shoulder, wrapping her arms around my waist. As her breath caressed my neck, I wondered if this was good-bye.

Soon, someone would come looking. My stepfather or the army brats—one of them would hunt us. Unlike Oliver and Kady, I was used to being pursued. This was the closest feeling I had to normalcy.

When I'd first found this cabin, it was a dark night without rain. I had stumbled in from the woods. My eyes stung from the vinegar my stepfather had tossed into them. My scraped knees and bloodied hands couldn't have taken another fall. This place had been my sanctuary. The end times had begun, and my stepfather had made one thing clear: this hunt was to end in my death.

I had found the water pump and washed myself off. My throat was dry, but I knew better than to drink the water without boiling it. The door had no lock, and the cabin had no electricity. I stumbled inside, with only the dim light from the moon shining through the windows.

I knew it wouldn't be long before Kyle and Zeke found me. Alongside one of the cabin's walls were iron traps—teeth strong enough to hold fast but not intended to kill. They would do fine. I grabbed three fox traps and set them up outside. Then I ran back inside, grabbed three more, and set them on all sides of the cabin. I shivered, but I forced myself to carry on.

To earn my place at the table, to prove to my stepfather that I was more than just bait, I had to turn from hunted to hunter. Inside the cabin, I found a warm plaid jacket that was two sizes too big. I wore it anyway and climbed up onto the roof. From there, I sat watching the woods for movement.

Oliver came up and sat close beside me. Unlike that day when I had waited for Kyle and Zeke, I wasn't shivering—but she was. She clutched her crossbow with white knuckles. Her breaths rasped in her lungs.

"Do we have a plan?" she asked.

"You shouldn't be up here. You're still sick."

Children of Ruin

I had never hated my stepfather as much as I did at that moment. He could have left me alone, and our two colonies could have coexisted without trouble. My life could have been peaceful. I was just starting to understand what that meant. And what did Oliver think of all this? Did she regret finding me, putting her trust in me? The silence between us was long, but I didn't know how to end it.

"None of this is your fault," she whispered in my ear, as if she knew my thoughts. "I'm okay now. Weak, yes, but fine."

Her voice echoed against what was once a lost memory. I had been waiting on the roof for my stepfather's sons to find me. It had felt like hours passed before I heard the first rustling of bushes. Something rustled in the bushes toward the cabin, slowly but steadily. It wasn't a loud rustle, and had I not been listening intently, it would've blended in with the crickets and frogs of the woods. But I had been listening. I had been waiting.

Zeke had stepped out into the clearing, alone. He was shaking, but not from fear. He shook from the adrenaline rush that came with the hope of winning the hunt. I felt it, too as I stayed crouched low until I knew for certain that he was alone. I stood and tapped my shoe against the roof so that it would sound like a woodpecker. Zeke looked up at me and smiled. He did not call to the eldest, no doubt wanting this victory alone.

Which was what I had counted on.

Zeke kept his gaze locked on me as he paced around the cabin. If I bolted, he'd have no trouble cutting off my escape. I didn't run. Had no intention of running. I was leading him. Coaxing him. The metallic chink of the spring was loud enough that I could hear it from my perch, but before Zeke could look down at his footing, a fox trap clamped shut around his ankle. He screamed once, and in unison I howled with my head tilted back. As I'd hoped, nearby wolves howled along with me, masking Zeke's pleas. I didn't see him fall, didn't see his head hit the sod, didn't see the bear trap that sprang shut around his neck. But I didn't want to see the first person I had ever killed die such a horrible death.

Now, once again, I sat on top of the roof—though this time I wasn't alone. Oliver rested her head on my shoulder, and I felt emotions that I had turned off long before. They sparked alive like tiny firecrackers. The three of us could just flee, head south and start again. I considered it.

"We can't run," I said out loud, knowing Oliver was thinking the same thing.

"Why not? Does the house mean that much to you?"

The house. Where I grew up. Where my mother planted her gardens. Where my sister played on her swing. Where my stepsiblings tortured me, and my stepfather brought me to the shed for re-education.

"The house can burn to the ground for all I care," I said without emotion. With a touch of anger, I added, "But there will be many left in this world who are like my stepfather. If we always run, one of them will eventually catch us."

We spoke no more words that night. No more words were needed. Memories of my stepbrother as he bled out filled my mind. But what I remembered most were Kyle's blood-curdling screams as he stumbled from the woods.

Children of Ruin

His wails were like calls to my stepfather, and I took them as my declaration that I had finally won. Back then, I couldn't have cared less as I prepared for what my stepfather would do to me. But then again, when I had watched Kyle weep for the loss of his younger brother, my heart swelled with pride that I had won.

That night the rooftop had become my sanctuary. It was the seat I had taken to move through the ranks of my stepfather's army. *No one could know of this place*, I'd decided as I picked up my bow. Kyle was still weeping, his face buried deep in his dead brother's chest. He only looked at me when I let out a slight whistle. I had wanted him to see the arrow that would kill him. I had wanted him to see me fire it. I had wanted to watch him die.

On that day, three boys died.

Oliver slept beside me as I pondered all the things that had happened that day. She had just fallen asleep, so I didn't wake her for her watch. Tears had streaked her mud-caked cheeks. Her hair, though still short, had grown back in as matted blond locks. If I failed her, if I couldn't protect her, then again the fear of what might happen to her, the fear that had driven her to become "Oliver," might well become real. Just thinking about it, I welled up with anger. *If fear didn't grip on me that night so many months ago, it needn't have a grip tonight*, I thought.

Because of her, I was no longer dead. All those emotions I had shut off now flooded back into me. At first I worried they would make me weak, and with them I would be too scared to fight back. Now, as I watched her chest rise and fall with deep breaths, I needed them to win.

"Wh-what time is it?" she mumbled as her eyes flitted open.

"It's morning," I said flatly.

"Why didn't you wake me? Did you sleep?"

"No. I don't need it."

"You aren't Batman." Her hand rubbed my back in small circles. I wondered if it was wrong that I still didn't feel sadness that the world had fallen. As she rested against me with her head on my shoulder, I thought this might have been the best moment of my life.

"I'm going to kill my stepfather today."

"I know. I'm coming with you. So will Kady. She's ready."

"You aren't. She isn't. This has to be between him and me."

Her head lifted off my shoulder, and I felt her stare on me. I couldn't look at her. She couldn't know how scared I was.

"And she and I will do what? Stay here and watch the homestead?"

"No. You're both going to run far away, and you're going to live."

"Without you, I am going to live alone."

A week. A month tops. That's how long Oliver and Kady would last without finding a colony they could trust. To find out if they could trust someone was a big chance to take. Fall asleep. Hope they wake up alive. Every night they would have to learn again: could they trust anyone? I wished Connor were with us so he could protect them.

"You two will look out for each other."

"But I want *you*!" Her hands cupped my cheeks, and she forced me to look at her. "You don't expect to come back alive, do you?" Her voice had that tone I had once heard in my mother's just before my real dad died. Was it . . . remorse?

"I expect to win," I said, as if that were an answer.

The first time I had waged war on my stepfather, when I'd lured his sons to the cabin and then attracted the soldiers to his home, I had also expected to win. And maybe I had or I hadn't won, considering the soldiers hadn't killed him. But because they had driven him from the colony, I got stronger.

"Do you hear that?" Oliver whispered, and I heard it for the first time. At first I heard a gentle rustle of bushes. But soon the snapping of twigs turned into a crashing through the woods.

They had found us. Unprepared. We were dead.

CHAPTER TWENTY-FOUR

Oliver loaded her crossbow at the same moment that I loaded my bow. She grunted as she pulled the drawstring back, and I knew she wouldn't be able to do that twice. We steeled ourselves for either my stepfather's army or the army brats, knowing no matter which showed up, this would be our last stand.

Kady better be prepared. Just in case, I kicked my foot on the roof as an alarm for her. We had nowhere to hide. Nothing to crouch behind. What had I been thinking? That this would be a safe place? I should've set the traps around the cabin. In the end, we would take more than a few with us.

The first of the army emerged, and I nearly released my arrow. He was dressed in camouflage but not wearing a flak jacket. His face was gray, and rotted skin hung from his cheeks. Then they all emerged, and they all had that same look. Decomposed bodies that shouldn't be wandering the woods. But they were. The army brats had released their ultimate weapon and had aimed it straight for my stepfather's colony. That meant Timothy was walking with them somewhere, probably at or near Evergreen Resort.

This is how I will win. I understood now. The same way

Timothy thought he would win. I understood the power he wielded, and the events played out in my mind. I saw what I had to do, and what it would take to end the war with my stepfather. I had been a blind boy wandering the land of the One-Eyed King. But in the land of the blind, I saw how I would steal the reign of the One-Eyed King.

"General, what are you thinking?" Oliver asked me. She was gripping my arm tightly, and I suspected she knew what I was about to do.

Images of my mother flooded into my mind, of how sometimes she'd hated my stepfather and sometimes she'd loved him. Before his accident, they had been affectionate with each other. They found sitters for us kids while they went on dates, and they often kept their bedroom door locked at night after they thought we'd gone to sleep.

During his recovery, she bought my stepfather novels to read. When he became obsessed only with conspiracy stories, she fed into it by bringing him all that he asked for. Then she listened to him ramble on for hours about the storylines—not seeing that point when he no longer believed they were fictional. In losing his eye, the words he had read turned to voices of prophetic wisdom. Conversations that had scared my mother. Yet, perhaps because she still loved him, she listened and never argued.

Oliver was trying to look me in the eyes, just as my mom had once done with my stepfather. How that made it easier to read someone, I couldn't understand. I liked Oliver, always had, and it was never a mixed-emotions kind of feeling. Whether she was Oliver or Olive had made no difference to me. At this moment, my emotions were sadness—a strange yearning to not go where I couldn't return.

I brought my hand up to Oliver's cheeks, the way she had done to me when we first met on the credit union's rooftop. She let loose her grip on my arm and brushed my cheek with the back of her fingers. I was sad that only now I understood what these motions meant.

She closed her eyes. Leaned in closer.

I leaped to my feet and jumped from the roof. It was not high enough that I needed to worry about the fall, but I did land harder than I had expected. I stumbled and made a racket as I banged into a pile of fire logs. A nearby deader turned to me just as Oliver yelled, "NO!"

The deader fell after a *thwapt!* and a bolt appeared in his forehead.

"Oliver, save your ammo!" I told her.

She didn't listen to me. She never had before, so why would she now?

I scoured the area for another deader. They weren't hard to find. They ran at me, and I ran back at them. Each time, Oliver shot them in the head.

"Please, Ethan! Get back up here!"

"ETHAN!" Kady screamed at me from the cabin. I glanced one last time at Oliver on the roof to say goodbye, and at Kady, who watched through the window. I couldn't listen to them beg. I had to stay completely focused on my plan.

Deaders walked toward me out from the darkest, thickest part of the woods. Oliver wouldn't be able to shoot them. Rushing into the woods, I found myself in front of a cluster. My plan was ready for action, and once in motion I couldn't turn back. For a second, I wanted to forget my stepfather and leave with Oliver and Kady. Live that life of freedom without fear of rival colonies.

Children of Ruin

I heard a deader behind me and many more to the sides. I was surrounded and had now left myself no choice. Just like Doctor Manhattan in the *Watchmen* comics, I had to sacrifice myself to save my friends. Unlike what my mother showed my stepfather, I had no such love-hate for him. I just had hate.

With that, I rolled up my sleeve. A deader grabbed me from behind. I grabbed the deader by the hair and pulled his head onto my forearm. Another deader grabbed at my side, and then another. The deader whose hair I was holding bit down harder than I'd expected, and my blood burned as my whole body felt like it had caught on fire. Then, I could hear nothing but the beating of my heart as if it might shatter my eardrums.

All the deaders let me go and started wandering away. I drew my machete and stabbed into the brain of the one that had bitten me. I pulled my arm free and fell to the ground. I took out my first aid kit and poured antiseptic all over my wound. Lastly, I wrapped it with a bandage. I heard Oliver running toward me.

"That didn't help the girl we found," Oliver sobbed. "You'll die, too."

"But you'll live. And so will Kady," I whispered. "And the One-Eyed King will die."

I rushed through the woods, trying to put my burning blood to the back of my mind. From beneath the bandage, I could see my arm turning black, like a timer running down. A red line began making its way toward my heart. My blood had been poisoned. As I stumbled past the deaders, perhaps instinctually, they followed behind me. It made sense the corpses would be driven with me toward the living. The virus's primary objective was to spread.

I started to jog toward the farm to get there before I lost consciousness and died.

The deaders didn't follow as fast as I jogged, and I emerged onto the farm first. Bodies littered the field between the barn and the trees. Some were starting to rise again. I had to stop and take a moment to let the sight completely soak in. The army brats that had died were children, kids who had come to believe they could rule the world. The grown-ups who followed my stepfather should have protected them but instead stood over them in sick triumph.

A gibbet had been dragged to the middle of the field. Timothy screamed from inside it for someone to come save him. When I listened to his calls above the rest of the noise, I heard him calling for his mom. He was no longer the fearsome leader, no longer the dictator bent on controlling the region with an iron fist, but the child he had been before the virus poisoned the world. Before the virus poisoned him.

I approached the main building and got close enough to see the wooden shingle hanging above the door: Site Office. No longer a place for guests to check into their assigned cabins, it was now the headquarters from where the One-Eyed King planned his world takeover. Or at least his world around Loon Lake. I coughed and held my hand to my mouth, spitting blood into my palm.

Six men dashed from the house with rifles pointed at me. I took out my machetes, and forced myself to stand tall, even though all I wanted was to close my eyes and sleep forever. The clicking of their weapons was like crackles of fireworks. One of them fired, the gun blast igniting the air. But just as his finger pulled the trigger, my stepfather was on the stoop, knocking the barrel from proper aim. I was so numb that, had the bullet found me, I probably would not have felt it.

"You come back to die?" my stepfather yelled. His men kept their guns pointed at me.

"I came back to see if you are a coward," I said. I was shaking, but no longer from fear. The deader virus was pumping mercilessly through my veins.

My stepfather scoffed. "There's no dog here to save you."

The way he said this was the way I'd imagined Woundwort, the evil rabbit in *Watership Down*, speaking similar words to Bigwig. Everything I had lost because of him struck me all at once. Maybe this revelation was my white light at the end of the tunnel, or the song of angels calling me home. But it was as though I could sense my sister, my mother, Blake, Thomas, Connor, even my birth dad, all there with me. Their strength became my strength. They were giving me one last chance to beat the One-Eyed King.

Just then, the horde of deaders that had trailed behind me emerged from the woods. The men, focused on me, gave my stepfather nervous glances before he nodded at the deaders. The men rushed by me at what was obviously the more imminent threat: the zombies.

"When I took you and your mom in, I rescued you from financial ruin in the old world and from torture in this one."

"You killed her. You never rescued her!"

"Boy, you are but a newborn, blind, without the

Sight"—he gestured to his covered eye—"so how can I expect you to understand? Sacrifices had to be made by the weak so that the strong may endure."

My stepfather was fast. His foot slammed into my chest, sending me onto my back. I caught a glimpse of Timothy watching from the gibbet. He saluted me, as though to tell me he hoped I'd win. I attempted to stand, but fell back to the ground. The kick hadn't hurt me, as the deader virus was numbing my senses.

"You killed my boys." My stepfather walked around me, spitting on me as he spoke. I believed the regret I heard in him was real.

"You killed my mother. My sister," I said back.

"No." He laughed through gritted teeth. "You killed your sister. All I did was deliver her to you."

Hearing him speak of my sister sent a wave of anger through my blood. As though the deader virus had given me a super strength, I rose and uppercut my stepfather beneath the chin. He bit his tongue, and he cursed as his hand covered his bleeding mouth. I stood ready to fight.

The rain blanketed us, blinding us to the others like stage lights blinding an audience. Much like actors feel alone on the stage, it was as if he and I were the only two survivors in the whole world. But wasn't that the way it had always been? I remembered him teaching his sons, and me having to watch from a distance. I'd always credited him as having trained me, but that was only partially true. I had listened to the instructions he had given Kyle and Zeke, and had practiced them whenever no one was watching. Like the children of Sparta, I snuck from my room at night when everyone else was sleeping so that I could eat from the garden and easily master the skills that had come so hard to my stepsiblings.

"In the land of the blind—" my stepfather began.

"I was never blind." I interrupted. "You may have made me the one running in the woods, but I was never running blind. Nor am I running blind now."

My stepfather took out his machete and again we clashed. Sparks mixed with rain, but when he cut me I no longer felt it. The deader blood was numbing me, and as my foot smashed into his stomach, I hoped I had held out long enough to see this through.

He thrust with his blade. I sidestepped. A simple parry. And I grasped his wrist and twisted the knife from his fingers. He punched the back of my head repeatedly. But I couldn't feel it, so I didn't stop. My foot stomped his toes, and hooked behind his ankle. I threw him to the ground. Even as the blade of my machete arced down at his neck, I didn't see fear in him. I stopped just short of killing him.

"Do it!" he screamed. "Send me to my sons!"

I grabbed the sleeve of my coat and pulled it up over the bandage. Using the machete, I sliced off the gauze so my stepfather could clearly see the bite mark I had suffered.

"The virus is in me," I told him. Then, I bit down hard on his cheek. "And now it's in you!"

I stood and he screamed, catching the attention of other deaders. The dead were running low on the living and the virus needed to spread. At first they began walking toward us, but when the horde was all around us they did nothing but bump into each other and into my stepfather and me. I'd made my stepfather one of the dead.

He made one last rush at me as he turned crazy. He swiped with his machete, but I easily ducked and bobbed away. I kicked him back to the ground, and he reached out and grabbed my blade. Pulling it against his heart, he pressed but didn't push.

"You will rise as one of them." I spat blood at him as I shouted against the thunder and rain. Then I left him holding his palms to his ears and screaming. I wandered toward the water where I would also die and rise as one of them.

I collapsed, but hands caught me before I hit the ground. "No, you don't," a woman's voice said, and I wondered if it was my mother who had come back for me. Was she there to comfort me one last time? She placed me ass down on the sod and cupped my cheeks. My eyes fluttered open enough to see Kady, and I whispered, "Oliver? Where is Oliver?"

"At the boat. By the shore."

Behind me, I saw the shadowy figure of my stepfather lumbering toward us. I opened my mouth to scream a warning to Kady, to tell her to run, but either the words caught in my throat or the noise of the rain drowned them out.

Just as my stepfather towered over her and lifted his hands in fists, Kady grabbed my machete and spun around. She caught him off guard and sliced into his chest. He cried louder than the rainfall. Kady kicked him in the shins and kneed him in the jaw. He flew backward onto his back. Kady scooped me under the arm with her shoulder and helped me to my feet.

"You're not done yet!" she yelled. She walked me down to the banks, where I collapsed into the rowboat that Kady had waiting for us.

Oliver was there with a blanket around her. She was

shivering, and as Kady started the motor, Oliver grabbed my arm and rolled up my sleeve. The boat rocked as we pushed off and floated down the river. The engine roared to life just as a tiny needle pricked my arm. My eyelids fluttered.

"I've given you the intravenous medication we had left." Oliver's face changed from blurry to clear. "Maybe you'll live."

As the rain washed away the blood from my face, Oliver wrapped me in a blanket and held me close. Instead of numbness, I experienced pain. Every cut, scrape, bruise. As though I was being pummeled all over again.

But with that pain . . . came freedom.

Freedom from my stepfather.

Freedom with Oliver.

Books by James Alfred McCann

orca sports
FLYING FEET
JAMES McCANN

CHILDREN
OF RUIN

JAMES ALFRED McCANN

James McCann has written the popular novels *Rancor, Pyre, Renegade, Flying Feet,* and *Children of Ruin.*

He has written book reviews for the Canadian Children's Book News, and has taught countless workshops for hundreds of students.

Currently, McCann works with the Richmond Public Library as a digital services technician. While most of his time is spent writing, now and then he explores the open road in his Jeep, plays Dungeons and Dragons, or practices the ukulele.

Made in the USA
Columbia, SC
18 September 2018